SILVER SHIFTER

3

HER BEAR

JAMES & BOGLE

1

OWEN

God I loved that woman.

The morning after making love to Ariana for the first time, I wished I had convinced her to let me stay. I wanted to feel her in my arms, her small, warm body pressed up against me. To ask her if I could call her Ana, a nickname just for me, or what she liked for breakfast, or if she liked morning sex. But I understood why she hadn't stayed. She wanted to make a good impression on my family, and that meant not coming down for breakfast smelling like sex.

I sighed and rolled onto my back, staring at the ceiling. I don't think it was possible for Ariana to have made a better impression on my family. They loved her straight away—especially Mom.

A smile tugged at my lips. I couldn't help it. Seeing Ariana among my clan was satisfying in a whole new way. She belonged here. She'd make an amazing mate and an amazing mother one day. Even though our kids wouldn't be mine by blood, any child of Ariana's would be a child of mine. I'd love them just as much as I loved their mom.

The pounding of footsteps throughout the house told me it was time to rise. I was used to getting up early. To run a clan, you had to be an early riser. My dad had taught me that. Get up with the day and embrace it like it was your last.

I swung my legs over the side of the bed and stood. After a quick shower and change of clothes, I headed downstairs. My heartbeat sped up as I entered the kitchen, the scent of bacon and eggs luring me in. I inhaled, and my stomach rumbled. My bear growled in agreement, ready to be fed.

Even though I'd told Ariana to sleep in, I hoped she wouldn't. I couldn't wait to see her today. I wanted to kiss her and pull her against me. I wanted to sit and have breakfast with her and my family, to block out the rest of the world for a while.

But my mate was nowhere to be seen when I entered the kitchen. Mom leaned over the stove, grilling leftover potatoes from last night and stirring scrambled eggs while my nieces ran around her legs.

I chuckled as Mom shook Kimberly's youngest boy off her leg for the second time. "You have your hands full this morning," I said as I plucked Ben from Mom's ankle.

She looked over her shoulder, relief flashing in her eyes as I heaved Ben into my arms. "Thank you, Owen. Kimmy's cleaning up outside and left the kids with me until breakfast."

"How nice of her." I flashed a grin, and Mom swatted me with the end of her spatula.

"I could send you off to help her, you know," she threatened.

I raised an eyebrow. "Then who would help you with the kids?"

"Touche." Mom shook the spatula and turned back to face the stove, leaving me to care for Ben and Samantha while she finished up breakfast.

I corralled the two unruly kids into the dining room. They raced around my feet while I set the table for ten. My brothers usually had breakfast with their wives, but Kimberly always came over with the kids. Dad would join us soon, and then there were our visitors. We'd have a full dining room today—Mom's favorite kind.

A swift knock at the front door had me pausing, dishes in hand. Before I could answer, the door swung open.

"Good morning," Maximus said in the other room.

I set the dishes down and leaned through the dining room doorway. "Morning," I said. I glanced over the wolf alpha's shoulder and out through the front door. No sign of Ariana. Damn.

"Good morning, dear," Mom said. "How did you sleep?"

"Well, thanks," Maximus said, shifting awkwardly. His gaze roamed the kitchen, then the dining room, searching for the same someone I was hoping would show up any minute now.

"She's not here yet," I said.

His disappointed expression reflected my own. "Anything I can do to help?"

"We're almost set up." I finished sorting the cutlery before I returned to the kitchen. If Ariana wasn't with Max, then she had to be with Cash. Hopefully the two of them would arrive soon.

"Breakfast is ready," Mom sang out. "Why don't you get Kimberly and Dad from the backyard?"

"Sure thing." I crouched in front of Ben and Samantha, who both peered at me with large blue eyes, looking exactly like younger versions of Kimberly. "Why don't you go wrestle Uncle Maximus while I get your mom and grandpa?"

Ben grinned from ear to ear while Samantha glanced at the wolf alpha with a mischievous glint in her eyes. Before Maximus could stop them, both kids had latched onto his legs, their chubby arms gripping his knees with bear strength.

"Owen," Maximus groaned. He teetered as he tried to remove Ben and Samantha, but I caught a hint of a smile on his lips. "What am I supposed to do here?"

I chuckled as I opened the back door. "Just watch them for a minute."

Before I heard Maximus's reply, I stepped outside, letting the door close behind me. Kimberly and Dad were picking up leftover trash from last night's festivities, occasionally tossing a crumpled beer can to the other's area when they weren't looking.

My chest swelled at the sight of my family. I hadn't been home nearly as much as I liked in the last few weeks, but it was nice to see that nothing had changed. Home was always waiting for me when I returned. I took great comfort in that.

"Breakfast is ready!" I called.

They stopped what they were doing and turned. Kimberly's cheeks turned red, embarrassed at having been caught. She was the last to throw a beer can. Dad only laughed as he wheeled up the ramp I'd built onto the side of the porch. I held open the door for Dad and Kimberly, who paused a moment to lean her half-full garbage bag against the side of the house.

"It smells great, Mom," Kimberly said as she entered the house.

I closed the door behind us and followed them into the dining room.

Maximus sat on one side of the table, Samantha in his lap and Ben bouncing up and down on the chair beside him. Cash sat on the other side of the table, a wide grin on his face.

My eyebrows furrowed as I inhaled, searching for

Ana's jasmine scent. It was there, but faint, probably from yesterday.

Maximus and Cash both took a second to glance around the room before they stiffened at the same time I did. We all knew who was missing—our mate.

I turned on my heel and strode back into the kitchen. "Mom, have you seen Ariana this morning?"

Mom looked up, her forehead wrinkled in confusion. "No, not yet."

I turned to my sister as my heart began pounding. "Kimberly?"

"Not since last night," Kimberly said.

"Don't worry, dear," Mom said. "She's probably slept in. I'm sure she needs it."

Maximus and Cash were on their feet and in the kitchen in moments.

"Who saw her last?" Maximus asked, a growl edging his voice.

"I haven't seen her since last night at the cookout," Cash said.

They both looked at me. I tilted my chin up slightly. There was no reason to feel ashamed of sleeping with my mate. "I saw Ana in her room last night, but I left not long after midnight."

Maximus narrowed his eyes and ground his teeth, but Cash simply nodded. There was no judgment in his eyes, no anger or jealousy. Cash was already thinking ahead, not dwelling on what had happened.

"She wasn't in her room when I got up," Kimberly said, joining us with Ben on her hip.

"Then where the hell is she?" Maximus snapped. I understood his agitation all too well. We may not have been childhood friends like Jett and Cash, but Maximus and I had a lot in common. We'd each taken over our respective clans at an early age, and neither of us had been ready for it. And now we had something else in common—an irresistible instinct to protect our mate.

I took a deep breath, trying to rein in the terror that sent my pulse racing. She might have gone out for a walk. Maybe she didn't know to come look for us in Mom and Dad's house. Maybe she'd slept in.

"Kimberly, double check your house, please," I said. This wasn't the time to panic, but it was the time for action. A plan quickly formed in my head as I barked out orders. "Maximus, check the surrounding area. Cash, check my house."

I hardly got the words out before Maximus and Cash were out the door, and Kimberly was depositing Ben at our mother's feet.

"I'm sure she's fine, Owen," Kimberly said. She laid a gentle hand on my arm. "I'll be right back."

I nodded and took a few calming breaths, centering myself. "I'm coming with you."

Kimberly raised her eyebrows but said nothing, only nodded as she led the way to the door. I followed on her heels, but five minutes later, it was clear Ariana wasn't in Kim's house.

I slammed my fist on the kitchen counter as Kimberly descended the stairs back to the first floor. "Where is she?"

Kimberly's nostrils flared as she slipped by me. She sniffed the air in the kitchen, around the fridge, and then walked to the rarely used breakfast nook. On the small window bench were several shreds of chicken and a glass of water that had tipped over. It dripped off the ledge onto the floor, forming a small puddle.

"She was here," Kimberly said. She pointed at the windowsill and then continued to test the air. "I don't smell anyone else, but there's something here..."

I joined her between the breakfast nook and the kitchen island, inhaling deeply. Chloroform. My heart raced as I scanned the floor—the water dripping from the window bench, the bits of chicken. That, coupled with the scent of chloroform confirmed it for me. Someone had taken my mate.

"Assemble everyone. We need to investigate every inch of the property." I hardly got the words out before racing out the back door. There were footprints in the dirt with deep grooves like some kind of hiking boot.

"I'm on it!" Kimberly called as she raced back to Mom and Dad's house.

Maximus ran up, his chest heaving. "Did you find her?"

I shook my head. "There were signs of a struggle."

Max's eyes flashed gold, and a growl rumbled in his throat. "The vampires took her. I'll fucking kill them."

I grabbed Maximus's arm before he could run off. "We don't know that," I said. Despite the panic swirling inside me, I tried to breathe through it and think rationally. Someone had to. "Do you smell any vampires?"

Maximus paused, his mouth half open to argue. Then he grimaced and shook his head.

"Then let's follow Ariana's scent. Maybe we'll get some answers," I said.

Maximus regarded me for a long moment before nodding.

Using both of our keen senses of smell, we followed Ariana's trail through Kimberly's garden to the edge of the forest.

Cash raced to catch up with us, pausing to catch his breath when he met us. "Anything?"

"We're following her trail," I said. "Come on."

I led the way into the forest. The footprints helped, leading the way deep into the trees until a small clearing opened up. I skidded to a halt at the edge.

Half a dozen pairs of footprints trampled the dirt around a set of tire tracks. Someone had taken our Ana, and someone was going to pay.

As I stared down at the boot prints in the dirt, my mind raced with a thousand possibilities and regrets. I had let Ariana go the night before, had let her have her space against my better judgment. Now she was gone. I thought of how she must feel, alone and scared out there somewhere. My wolf exploded toward the surface of my mind, rage fueling him as he clawed for control. He was right. He could scent her, find her pack link, track her down. We'd follow her to the end of the earth and kill the fucking coward who had stolen her in the night.

"Maximus," Owen said, laying a massive paw on my arm. "This isn't the time to lose control."

"It's the exact right time to lose control," I snarled. "Don't you care that they took Ariana? We need to find her *right fucking now*."

Owen blinked at me, his eyes dark with anguish.

"Of course we care," he said. "That's why we need to do this rationally. So we can all get our mate back."

For the first time since Ariana said the words to me, they didn't sting. It wasn't personal now. Her having three mates wasn't a rejection of me and my wolf. It was our best hope. Having four mates was the biggest advantage she had right now. These men wouldn't just try to get her back because she could unite our clans and make political peace. They would fight to the death for their mate, just as I would. My gaze moved between the other two men, fur rippling along my arms and claws extending from my fingertips.

"Then let me track her," I said, my teeth aching as they threatened to lengthen into fangs. I couldn't remember the last time I'd come this close to losing control of my wolf. He seemed determined to tear free of my grip and run like a wild animal, hunting down our mate and the vermin who took her.

"Keep your head," Owen said. "We can't communicate with you in wolf form."

That was it. I could communicate with Ariana. I closed my eyes, willing my wolf to quiet so I could hear her.

"What's he doing?" Cash asked. "If he can't go after her, I will."

"Just shut up and let me see if I can find her through our pack bond," I growled, renewing my concentration.

At last, I felt her. It was faint, as if she were far from me. But our pack bond could not be broken. We'd claimed each other. She was mine. There was no way for her to erase the pack bond now. The only thing that could sever the bond was death.

"She's alive," I breathed, my chest bursting with relief. The other two men looked as nervous as I felt as they waited for more. I wanted to tell them she was fine and not far away. I wanted to share something good with them. Instead, I had to shake my head. "I can't feel anything else. She's alive, but there's nothing else. She must be sleeping."

"Or knocked out," Owen said. "The chloroform..."

I gave a quick nod. It was true. I could feel her there, but I couldn't read a single thought. It was the usual pattern for someone unconscious. Unfortunately, there was no way to tell if it was sleep or something more sinister that was keeping my mate subdued.

Our mate.

I met Owen's tortured gaze and Cash's frantic one.

"There's no way to know," I admitted, reining my wolf in again. "But even if she's just sleeping, that doesn't make it better. She could have worn herself out fighting all night. She didn't go willingly."

"Ariana never would," Owen rumbled, a tiny, sad smile tugging at his lips.

"I'll fly over and see if I can see where this road

goes," Cash said. "Maybe they haven't gone too far. We don't know when they took her."

"This road winds around for quite a while," Owen said, scratching his beard. "All the way through the valley. They can't drive fast on it, either. It's gravel the whole way."

Maybe, just maybe, there was hope. I clenched my fists, aching for it to be true—aching for her to be okay. She had to. My mind reeled with the thoughts of all we hadn't done yet. I'd waited ten years for my mate, and I'd barely claimed her before she was taken from me. I'd only made love to her once. We'd never had a chance to play together, to run as wolves together, or hunt together. I'd pictured a long life with her, one full of pups and laughter. I'd wanted to let down my guard with her, to let her in.

But I hadn't.

The night we'd spent together as mates, she'd told me she loved me, and I hadn't even said it back.

While I was brooding over my loss, Cash peeled off his clothes and spread his wings, taking off before he'd finished shifting into dragon form.

"I have to do something," I said, grabbing my head with both hands as if I could shake her awake through our bond. "I can't just stand around while some fucking vampire is holding my mate hostage."

"It could be Dante," Owen said. "Since it doesn't smell like vamps, maybe her master came back for her."

Rage swelled inside me, and my wolf rippled toward the surface again. Dante had kept her prisoner for years, forcing her to fight for her life and his entertainment. He'd hurt my mate, almost broken her, before I rescued her from his clutches. I'd let him get away that time. If he'd snuck in and stolen her in the night, I wasn't going to make that mistake again. When I'd found her, I'd been so anxious to get her to safety that I hadn't gone after him. She'd been my number one priority from the moment I laid eyes on her.

That might change the next time I saw the warlock.

"We should check both Dante and the vampires," I said. "We can call Jett to check on the vamps. He's got all those connections and spies."

Just then, Cash appeared over the treetops and skidded to a stop amid a cloud of dust and pebbles. He shifted partially, his wings still extended. "I lost her," he growled. "The trail ends when the dirt road meets the highway. Too many cars have passed since she was taken."

"Then it must have been sometime in the middle of the night," Owen said. "There's not a lot of traffic on that highway. A half dozen cars might pass in an hour."

"Over four or five hours..." I said, thinking of all the cars that had worn away the scent of the tires we needed. Cars that had passed, their occupants oblivious to what they were doing. We'd just have to find her some other way. Whatever it took, we would do it. We would never stop until we got our mate back. They'd erased Ariana's trail, but no matter what anyone did to her or to us, they could never erase her from our hearts.

3

ARIANA

The soft click of a door broke through the fog of sleep encasing me. I shifted on the hard metal digging into my spine. I tried to call back the memories of what had happened, but the pounding in my skull scrambled them like eggs. My tongue was heavy in my mouth, which was filled with a nasty coppery taste. My throat ached along with my temples, beating in rhythm with my heart.

I groaned and reached for my head, clutching my hair as another bite of pain shot through it. Slowly, I curled onto my side to wait out the pain and fog.

After what felt like an hour but had probably only been a few minutes, I risked opening my eyes. Bright overhead light speared my skull. I squeezed my eyelids closed and pressed my palms against my eye sockets. Something about this was familiar. Flashes of a human face with rugged facial hair and ruddy, pocked skin flashed behind my eyes.

Humans.

My heart skipped, and my eyes flashed open. Humans had done this. All this time, we'd thought it had only been vampires after me, but humans were getting in the game now, too.

Fuck me.

A growl rumbled in my throat. My fists tightened, and hot anger flared through my chest. As I moved to sit up, I realized the haze in my mind wasn't clearing. Though my anger normally woke beastie from her slumber, she was silent in head. My heart raced as I searched for my wolf, but she too remained distant.

"What the hell?" I hissed. Panic gripped me. They couldn't be gone. They were as much apart of me as my arms or legs. And yet, when I called them, I only felt the faintest brush of my beasts in my mind.

Gritting my teeth, I finally sat up. I was in a metal room that felt more like a cage. There was a mirror on one side, almost half the size of the wall, and a door stood on the far side. Besides a small commode in the corner, the room was otherwise barren.

I was captured *again*. I'd spent almost my entire life in a cage, and now I was back in one. Unlike my previous cell, at least I could get up and move around without my shoulders pressing against steel bars. I slid off the table at the center of the room. Cold metal met my toes, and I recoiled. They'd taken my shoes and my clothes. Instead of the pajamas I'd gone to bed in, I was dressed in a white tank-top and loose fitting white cotton pants.

Someone had *dressed me*. Which means someone took off my clothes. My skin crawled, and my body went cold. I shook myself and rubbed the goosebumps from my arms. I didn't want to consider how vulnerable I had been. They could have killed me, or worse. At least I was alive. That meant they needed something from me.

Steeling myself, I slipped off the table. I had to find a way out.

My heart pounded in my ears as I raced around the tiny room. I felt along the edges of the door, looking for a seam I could slip my fingernails under, but I couldn't find any. Next, I inspected what looked like a keypad beside the door. It was too tight to the wall, and I couldn't get a grip on the underside of the metal box.

An irritated growl rumbled in my throat, echoing in the quiet room. I tried the mirror next, but it was embedded in the wall. After a good fifteen minutes of inspecting my new prison, I resigned myself to the fact that there was no easy way out.

Whoever wanted me, I was theirs. But what would humans want with a shifter?

I closed my eyes and inhaled slowly, trying to get my rational mind back in place. This was not the time to freak out, no matter how tempting it might be.

Again, an image of the human in the back of that van flashed through my mind. What had he said? They'd been looking for me for a long time. But why? I ground my teeth, trying to pull back the memory.

Before I could, a click echoed through the room.

My heart jumped. Instinctually, I slipped to the far side of the room, putting the table that was anchored to the floor between myself and my captor.

The door slid into the wall like some kind of science fiction movie. A woman with white hair tied up into a messy bun appeared on the other side. She had metal rimmed glasses balanced on the tip of her nose, barely holding on with her head tipped down to the clipboard in her hands. As she stepped over the threshold into my cell, she finally looked up. Blue eyes met mine and widened with delight.

"Ariana. You're awake," she said, her voice breathy. "You shifters are far more resilient than I suspected."

I narrowed my eyes at the petite woman eyeing me with a mixture of awe and scholarly intrigue. "Who are you?" I demanded. Again, I reached for the beasts inside me, but they were strangely quiet.

Her lips parted in a surprised 'o'. "Oh, forgive me. How rude of me not to introduce myself!"

The woman took a step forward, clutching her clipboard to her chest. She wore a long white lab coat, so I assumed she was some kind of scientist or doctor. What did a human doctor want with me?

"I am Doctor Muriel Siegfred, head researcher for

the Human Conservation Association, or HCA. I specialize in supernatural species and phenomena."

I blinked slowly at her. None of that meant a thing to me. A flurry of questions filled my mind, but first and foremost, why the hell had they kidnapped me?

Muriel's lips pressed together in a firm line. "Apologies, Ariana. I'm sure this is all very overwhelming. We didn't mean to scare you, but the very survival of the human race is at stake here."

"Um... What now?" I raised an eyebrow.

She nodded gravely. "Supernaturals of all species have been growing exponentially over the last hundred years, I'm sure in reaction to our own growing population." Muriel took another step inside. "HCA was created to assess and research the supernatural world while also guarding the secret from the human population. Can you imagine if word got out that shifters and vampires were real? There would be mass hysteria."

I narrowed my eyes. "What does that have to do with me?"

Muriel's gaze lit up. "That, my dear, is the winning question. First, allow me to explain. While shifters and witches have never opposed humans directly, vampires feed on our kind." Her grip tightened on her clipboard. It looked like Muriel liked vampires about as much as I did. "I've searched for a cure for vampirism for the last twenty years, to no avail. Then, I receive word that vampires who had attacked a young shifter had reverted to their natural human state. I couldn't believe my ears—until I saw one for myself."

The longer she spoke, the faster my heart beat. I didn't like the delighted look on her face or the crazy glint in her eyes. "You want to use me," I said flatly.

Of course she did. I was so not surprised by her explanation. I'd been a commodity for most of my life. Only Maximus had saved me from that. Only he and my other mates had wanted me as anything more than a weapon in their games.

"That's not a very nice way to put it." Muriel cleared her throat and adjusted her glasses. "But in a sense, yes, we want to use your blood to cure vampirism once and for all."

I could see the future Muriel spoke of. I'd be locked in this cell, forced to donate blood or bone marrow or whatever the fuck they wanted until I died. As a shifter, I would heal quickly with every needle in my vein. There would be no life for me, only a long, torturous death. And for what? To cure a bunch of vampires who probably wanted to remain what they were as much as humans wanted to stay human?

I didn't like vampires any more than the next person, but these humans wanted to annihilate an entire species. What would be next? My chest squeezed painfully. What about my mates, their clans, and their families? Would the humans try to destroy them, too? Maybe wolves didn't want to drink their blood, but they wanted territory. What happened when humans decided we were encroaching on their land, or that they wanted to build a subdivision in the bears' beautiful valley?

I shook my head. I couldn't let them do this. I had to get out of here.

I took a step forward, and Muriel instantly backpedalled. At some point the door had swished closed behind her. I inspected her white lab coat until I found a plastic identification card attached to her pocket. There was a barcode along one side. Maybe that would work on the panel beside the door.

My pulse sped as I approached the doctor. Muriel blanched, her eyes wide as she backed against the wall.

"A-Ariana? What's wrong?"

I slammed my palm against the door, inches from her head. "I'm a prisoner, that's what. Now, you're going to let me out of here, *Doc.*"

"I-I can't do that."

My lips pulled back in a snarl. Somewhere deep in my belly, Beastie rolled over, awakening from her slumber. "Wrong answer."

I grabbed the keycard from Muriel's coat.

She made a grab for her card, but I had her wrist in my hand before she could blink. I pulled hard, yanking the doctor off of her feet. She crumpled to the floor as I lunged for the panel.

I swiped her keycard over the small metal box,

relief crashing through me as it blinked green and beeped cheerfully. My heart leapt as the door whooshed open.

"Wait!" Muriel called.

Too late.

I was already leaping through the door—and right into a hallway full of armed guards. My nostrils flared as the scent of humans filled my head. Beastie rumbled inside me, and heat consumed my chest.

I had no idea where I was, or how I was going to get out, but fuck if I was going to stay. I was getting the hell out while the getting was good.

As a dozen assault rifles lifted in my direction, I let my anger fill me. My beast roared to life, her scales forming on my arms and smoke filling my mouth.

Pain slammed into my skull, halting my transformation. I fell to the floor with a grunt. Darkness speckled the edges of my vision, pulling me towards unconsciousness.

"You all right, Dr. Siegfred?" someone asked.

Muriel sighed and crouched over me. "I'm fine, but it looks like our patient won't be quite as cooperative as we thought. On to plan B."

Plan B?

My mind raced to make sense of what I had just heard, but before I could get out a word, a sharp pain pierced my shoulder as a needle pricked my skin, and once again, darkness overtook me.

4

ARIANA

I crouched in a tree, watching my mates race around in the forest below, calling my name. I opened my mouth, aching to answer them, but I couldn't make a sound.

I knew I was dreaming. I hadn't climbed a tree in years. Most wolves didn't like climbing, preferring to keep their feet on the ground instead, but I'd always loved it. I wished I'd gotten a chance to climb a tree the way I had as a kid, when my parents would watch my shenanigans with sadness in their eyes that I didn't understand. In my bid to keep their attention and erase the resigned sorrow I saw in the people I loved, I'd grown to be quite a daredevil.

But in the dream, I wasn't being daring and reckless, swinging from a high branch by my knees and calling for anyone to look at me. Instead, I was frozen, panic clawing at my throat. Why couldn't I speak?

I searched for the pack bond, finding it strong as Maximus called my name from just a few feet away. And because it was a dream, my parents were suddenly there, too. They were all calling. I found Maximus's strong Alpha signal and snatched at it.

"Maximus," I screamed in my head. *"I'm right here. Help me!"*

I woke with a start, sucking in a breath and trying to bolt upright.

Strong bonds gripped my arms, and I swore as I realized where I was.

Fuck. I was in a lab where humans planned to experiment on me. As if that weren't bad enough, now they were treating me like a criminal, chaining me to the bed. I jerked as hard as I could against the straps holding my arms and legs. Though they were padded so they didn't burn into my skin, I knew they were silver when I couldn't even begin to rip free of them.

Something else was wrong, though. What had they done to me? I felt so weak. Less than a minute of straining against my bonds left me slightly out of breath, and my throat burned every time I swallowed. And damn, why was I so tired?

Was this how humans felt when they got sick? Shifters didn't get common colds or other human ailments, and if this was how they felt, I wanted no part of it.

A shock went through me as an idea struck. If my

blood could make vampires human, what if their blood could make *me* human? Had the doctors injected me to see what would happen, and now I was a fucking human?

"Maximus," I whispered, pain needling my throat when I so much as whispered. I remembered my dream, though. I could use the pack bond. I called for Wolfie inside me, but she was cowering in fear. Still, I closed my eyes and concentrated, sending out feelers, reaching for my alpha. Where was he? He couldn't be close, because I couldn't find so much as a whisper of his signature. There was only silence where my pack had been.

Opening my eyes, I jerked at the straps again, letting out a furious scream despite the pain that went knifing down my throat when I did.

As if summoned by my banshee screams, the door slid open and the doctor appeared again.

"Ariana," she said, looking a little more wary this time than she had before. "You're awake. I'm glad to have you back with us."

"I bet you are," I snarled. "Now let me go, or you'll pay for this. My mates will find me. They won't stop looking until they do, and then you'll be sorry."

"I am sorry," Muriel said with a resigned sigh. "I don't want it to be this way. If you'd just cooperate, we wouldn't have to restrain you."

I bared my teeth at her. "Cooperate? What does that mean? Give you my blood until I'm weak and helpless? That's why I'm so weak, isn't it? You've been taking my blood."

"For now, we're only running a few tests," she said.

"Then what did you do to me?" I demanded.

"How about this," she said. "I'll answer your questions if you answer mine."

I narrowed my eyes at her. "What questions?"

I seriously doubted I knew anything that could help her, but I wasn't about to waste my chance at getting something in return. If she thought I knew something, I wasn't going to correct her unless it would get me out of there.

"We just want to know a few things about where you came from," she said.

"I'm from New York," I said. "And I don't need answers. I need freedom. Now untie my arms."

"Can you be more specific?"

"Can you take the silver chain off my right arm first, and then my left?"

She gave a slight smile. "I meant about where you were from."

"I answered."

"We already knew that," she said. "We're after new information."

"Fine," I said. "If you'll untie my arms, I'll give you my whole life story."

"And you won't attack me when I do?"

"No," I said. "I'm not an animal. I can control myself."

"Very well," she said. "Proceed."

"My parents belonged to a warlock, the father of one Dante Ryse. Maybe you've heard of him. He's a real gem."

She pulled a pen from her pocket and scratched something down on her clipboard. "You were born in captivity?"

"Yes," I said. "Their offspring were part of the bargain."

When I was young, I didn't understand the sadness I'd seen in my parents. As an adult, I understood it all too well. They hadn't wanted to bring a child into the world, knowing I would be owned by warlocks just as they had. But then I'd shown up, and they had loved me despite my unplanned existence.

"Did you have any siblings?"

I cut my eyes toward my arm and jerked my chin at it. Muriel sighed and reached beneath the armrest thing to snap open my cuff. She jumped back like I might attack her with only one arm free. I wasn't that crazy. "And this one?" I said, waving my left hand.

"Answer the question first."

"No," I said. "I don't have siblings. My parents didn't want kids, but I guess they slipped up one time. Lucky me."

"Lucky, indeed," Muriel said, noting something on her clipboard.

"Left hand."

She undid my other hand, and I rubbed my wrists in pure glee. I was almost free.

"What can you tell me about your parents?" she asked. "Did they have this special property in their blood?"

"I don't know," I said. "As far as I know, they didn't. Vampires don't usually bite wolves except in a fight. They don't like the taste of us any more than we like the taste of them. They don't feed on us unless they're trying to weaken us or kill us."

"So, your parents belonged to this warlock, and when he died, you were passed to his son Dante per the laws of supernatural property inheritance."

"Yes," I gritted out. I hadn't thought much about that growing up. Freedom had never been an option. Now that I'd had a taste of it, I realized the rest of the world didn't live by those laws.

"And your parents," she said. "They're no longer with us?"

"No," I said. "Sorry, you can't find them and harvest their blood, Doc. Now that you've got it all figured out, think you can untie my feet?"

"Your history could be very important," Muriel said. "It could lead us to more of you, if there's anyone else out there like you."

"Notice how I'm not jumping to join in on your crazy little plan?" I said. "You think I'm going to help you find someone else to kidnap and poison slowly with silver?"

"Well, if you'd cooperate, we wouldn't have to use that method to subdue you," she shot back.

I crossed my arms over my chest and glared. "I think I've given you enough information to warrant a few more chain removals, don't you?"

"I'm sorry to hear about your parents," Muriel said as she undid my feet. "That must have been a lonely time in your life."

"It was," I admitted with a shrug. "When Dante inherited us, he put my parents in the pits. They were good fighters, but eventually, everyone dies in the pits. It's not a matter of if. It's a matter of when."

"I'm sorry," Muriel said again, sinking onto the foot of the bed like we were settling in for a little chat. "I know this seems suspicious, but we don't want to hold you prisoner. Actually, we would love if you would join us."

"Join you?" I gaped at her. "This is how you recruit people to join your vampire fighting army?"

"We don't have an army," she said. "Unfortunately. You have to understand, Ariana. We're desperate. Vampires have killed thousands of humans. They are the ones with an army, waging war against a population that is practically defenseless."

I scrambled from the bed and stood facing her, wrapping my arms tightly around myself. "You seem pretty damn capable to me."

"The vampire plague isn't just hurting us," she said. "They've attacked you and your escorts several times this week. They attack shifters of all sorts as well as humans. They are a threat to life on earth. We would love to join with the shifter clans to fight their presence."

I had to admit she was right about that. All the vampires I knew were pretty evil. But that didn't mean they all were. Did it?

"We just want to take a bit of blood," she said. "If we can isolate what it is that's curing vampirism, it's possible that we can manufacture a synthetic alternative. We don't want to have to rely on one shifter to cure all of New York."

"And what if I don't agree?" I said, pressing my back to the wall. "What if I won't let you take my blood to clone whatever is getting rid of the vampires?"

"We hoped it wouldn't come to that," she said. "Don't you want to protect your pack and the other clans from these predators?"

I did. But at the same time, I wanted my freedom. I wanted it to be my choice. So much in my life had been decided for me.

"Not like this," I said. "Let me go, and then we can have a real negotiation."

She sighed and drew a syringe from the pocket of her lab coat. "I'm afraid that's not possible, Ariana. I'm going to ask one more time. Can I draw another sample?"

"No," I said. "You can't."

She didn't move from the bed or pull out a phone

to signal, but the next second, the door slid open and four hulking men entered the room and rushed toward me. I snarled, baring my teeth and leaping at them, calling on my wolf to come out and fight. She betrayed me, not even stirring inside me before the men had tackled me, pressing me back on the bed. I bucked and flailed, but one of them held my shoulders down. Another one wrapped a thick hand around my jaw, forcing my mouth open. A choked scream tore from my throat as he held a spray bottle to my lips. He pressed down, and a burst of fire shot down my throat. I screamed again, convulsing in agony this time.

"Colloidal silver," Dr. Siegfred said. "I'm sorry, Ariana. It's the only thing that keeps you subdued for us to extract what we need. Humans have to rely on such things when dealing with shifters. We don't have the natural advantages that you do." With that, she tapped on her syringe and plunged the needle into my arm. I watched redness swirl into the chamber, filling it higher and higher as my own rage swelled inside me.

"It's for the good of the world, if not for your own good," she continued. "We're still hoping you'll come around. In the meantime, we'll be studying your blood and trying to isolate the factor affecting the change from vampire to human. If we can find it, we'll let you go without any further harm."

As they left the room, I bent over the side of the bed, coughing and heaving. I wanted to throw up the silver, but I could already feel it seeping into my veins, making my body and mind sluggish, draining it of energy. No wonder my poor wolf wouldn't fight. They were killing her slowly, and she was too weak to fight back.

No further harm, my ass.

Even if Dr. Siegfred let me go, it was only me who would not be harmed more. What about the vampires? My only consolation was that I wasn't exactly killing the vampires. My blood just made them human again, brought them back to their original state. That wasn't so bad, was it?

I lay back on the bed, trying to wrap my head around what she wanted. Around what it really meant to be a cure for vampirism. I wasn't just a good fighter. I was a biological weapon.

5

CASH

I glanced at my companion in the passenger seat. Maximus glared at the brake lights flashing before us, a grim set to his jaw. His fists shook in his lap, his wolf so close to the surface I could nearly smell dog in my car.

"I swear, the moment I see that little weasel, I'm going to kill him," Maximus snarled through his teeth.

"You need to calm down, Maximus," I said. My fingers tightened around the steering wheel as I was forced to once again slow down for a red light. "You can't kill Dante before we get answers."

Maximus grumbled something I couldn't decipher, but at least he started taking even breaths. "I promised her she'd never have to go back to the pits, Cash. I promised her Dante would never hurt her again."

My chest clenched painfully, and it was my turn to fight for control. Heat coursed through me, and I bit my tongue when swaths of smoke rose from my nostrils. Maximus wasn't the only one close to shifting.

"And you'll keep your promise," I said. "We'll get her back."

Maximus only nodded. I could see the regret in his eyes, but at this point, there was nothing I could do to stop him from laying the blame on himself. He'd feel guilty until we had Ari back in our arms. Once she was safe, all would be forgiven.

"How do you think Owen and Jett are faring?" I asked, hoping to distract us both.

We'd called Jett and let him know what had happened after scouting Owen's valley. Since we couldn't be sure if it was Dante or vampires who had taken Ariana, we'd split up. While Maximus and I went after Dante, Owen and Jett were after the vampires.

Maximus growled. "I'm not worried about them."

A small smile tugged at my lips. "Jett is probably pissed that we tore him away from whatever he was doing. He sounded busy on the phone."

"Fuck him." The passenger door creaked where Maximus held the armrest. "He's always 'busy'. Maybe Ariana was right about him. What's his connection with the vampires again?"

My grin escaped at the bitterness in Maximus's tone. He'd never been a huge fan of my childhood friend. "He does seem to be preoccupied these days," I agreed. "But if anyone hates vamps, it's Jett."

Maximus grunted in agreement. Even he couldn't deny that Jett had the most personal hatred for vampires. They had killed his father, after all.

We drove in silence for the next few minutes until a neon sign caught my eye. *The Black Sparrow*. Maximus's wolves had tracked Dante to this club. From their descriptions, it sounded like Dante was up to his old tricks again. The stench of angry wolves and desolate shifters hung heavy on the place.

"That's it," Maximus said. "That's where she should be."

I ground my teeth just thinking about it. My mate was in there, being subjected to the Dragon God only knew what kind of hell.

"You're smoking," Maximus muttered.

I inhaled sharply. Sure enough, the vestiges of my smoky breath were just disappearing.

Across the street, the windows of the club were filled with vampires, shifters, witches, and supernaturals of all types. They schmoozed with glasses of liquor or blood, looking like they didn't have a care in the world. Behind them were flashing lights and a dimly lit bar interior. Outside was a line a mile long. It seemed The Black Sparrow was a popular spot.

"Let's go," Maximus said, unbuckling his seatbelt. "Ariana must be in trouble. If she's here, she's sedated somehow. I can't feel her through our bond at all."

I gave a quick nod before sliding into a parking spot directly across from the club. We climbed out,

Maximus slamming his door so hard a few pedestrians gave us concerned looks. I flashed a smile and hurried to catch up to the wolf alpha. "Don't cause a scene. Remember, we need to get to Dante. That means acting like we belong."

Maximus crossed his arms, hiding the claws that had extended from his fingers. He was straining so hard against his suit jacket, I swore I could hear the stitches ripping.

"Behave," I warned. Maximus was a little larger than me, and it would look funny to see a man walk into a place like that wearing ill-fitting clothes. No matter how hard it was, we had to play the elite shifters ready to see a fight in the pits. For the next few minutes, we weren't Ari's mates, we were just two guys looking for a good time.

Before heading toward the club, I locked the car doors, and my Mercedes beeped in response. I put on my best douchebag smirk and elbowed Maximus to remind him to do the same.

"Good evening," I said as we reached the bouncer.

"Back of the line," the large man grunted before he'd even taken a look at us.

The people at the head of the line stirred, grumbling about us trying to skip ahead. I cleared my throat to get the bouncer's attention. When the man sighed and turned to meet my gaze, I pulled two hundred-dollar bills from inside my jacket and slipped them into his hand.

"I'm sure this will be enough to get us inside," I said.

When the bouncer glanced down at the bills in hand, his eyes went buggy. He stepped back and held the door open for us even as a chorus of groans went up from the line. "Thank you, sir," he said. "Right this way."

I gave him a cocky smirk before stepping inside, Maximus hot on my heels. "Where should we start first? The bar?" When my companion didn't respond, I looked back over my shoulder. "What's wrong?"

Maximus stood stiffly, his eyes lit with rage. "I can smell the bastard," he growled through his teeth. His words were clipped, garbled by the fangs forming in his mouth.

"Maximus, calm yourself." I grabbed his arm and yanked him into a shadowed corner near the entrance. "We'll never get to Dante if you wolf out."

"I know," Maximus snapped.

"Do you smell Ariana?" I tried, raising my eyebrows for emphasis. "No. Because she's probably not here. So we need to get to Dante and find out if he has her."

Maximus's shoulders sank a fraction. "Good point."

I smirked. "As always."

Maximus glared daggers at me. "You might be having fun, but now is not the time to fuck with me."

I chuckled as I turned to face the rest of the bar.

After a quick scan, I noticed another bouncer standing at a door at the back of the long bar. The bouncer only let in a wealthy looking vampire couple in the time I watched.

"That's got to be it," Maximus said.

"I imagine so," I said. "Let's go for it."

Maximus frowned. "What happened to playing it cool?"

"That was only until we found the entrance. Now, we have to act like we belong in there." I nodded at the door. "Follow my lead."

I slipped through the crowd, Maximus following. I put my smirk back on and turned on the douchebag swagger. It worked well for intimidation, but from the narrowing of the bouncer's eyes, he wasn't fooled.

"Good evening," I said, stopping in front of the door that might lead us to Ari. My heartbeat picked up speed at the thought. Though I didn't smell our mate, I hadn't been able to smell whoever took her either. Maybe Dante had some sort of magic that could conceal her scent.

"Password?" the bouncer rumbled.

I yanked out a few bills. "Is this the correct password?"

The bouncer didn't even blink. "No."

I chuckled and slipped a few more from the bill-fold in my jacket pocket. "How about this?"

The bouncer only shook his head.

Maximus stepped forward, sending a shot of cold right into my gut. Shit.

Don't mess this up!

"Listen, we're old buddies of Dante's, and he told us to stop by when we could," Maximus said. "If you'll go get the boss man, I'm sure he'll vouch for us."

The bouncer's eyes turned into saucers, and his cold demeanor faded into fear. "Friends of the boss? My deepest apologies, gentlemen. I didn't mean to hold you up." The man stepped aside and held the thick red door open for us to enter a narrow stairwell leading down into the earth.

"Not a problem." I smiled as I slipped the bills I held into his breast pocket before following Maximus into the stairwell.

As soon as the door shut behind us, I breathed a sigh of relief, only to have my lungs filled with the stench of rage and fear. My skin crawled as the musky scent swirled through my head, threatening to drown me.

"We're definitely in the right place," Maximus said.

As I saw the muscle in his jaw twitch, his face twisting into a pained expression, I suddenly remembered where he'd found Ari. I tried to imagine the anguish I would have felt if I'd seen my mate in this place, a slave forced to murder to live. A whole new level of respect welled inside me, and I felt for Maximus in a way I hadn't before.

He'd already started down the steps, so I hurried to

follow. I had to switch to breathing through my mouth to combat the overwhelming stench. We descended the steps for a good minute before arriving at a sleek, square room cut from stone. Unlike the cavern Maximus had described, this new space was full of metal furnishings, glass countertops for the bar, and glowing lights behind the bottles nestled against the wall behind the bar. At the center of the large space was a giant cage. I could feel the crackle of magic in the air. Whatever those bars were made of, they had to be enchanted. I had a feeling that whatever breed of shifter touched those bars, they'd be left magic-burned.

A mountain lion prowled one edge of the massive cage while a tiny coyote was shoved through a dark entrance carved into the lone stone wall. The coyote shifter yelped and searched helplessly until its eyes landed on the mountain lion.

"Fuck," I cursed.

The crowd surged toward the cage, hooting and hollering, screaming for the blood of the coyote. The mountain lion snarled and hissed at the coyote, only spurring the cries of the crowd.

"Let the battle begin!" a man announced from the far side of the room.

Even as Maximus stiffened and yanked at my arm, I stood rooted to the floor. All of these people, be them witch, shifter, vampire, or something else altogether, were going to watch this. They *thrived* on the energy of the fight between these two shifters. How could they watch this, let alone condone it?

"Cash." Maximus squeezed my arm so tightly I winced. "I know it's hard, but you have to forget about them for the moment. We'll come back and free them all, but right now Ariana is the priority."

Ari. We were here for our mate. I shook myself. "Right."

"Come on," Maximus said as he pulled me through the crowd toward the opposite side of the room. "I smell Dante."

Slowly, I pulled back from the desolate feeling left inside me from seeing the caged shifters. No matter what, I was going to put a stop to this. But Maximus was right. Our mate came first.

As we slipped through the crowd, a VIP section came into view. Behind a red velvet rope was a small platform raised off the stone floor. Leather couches circled the platform, and a glass table sat at the center. On the largest sofa at the back sat a man with slicked back hair and a large grin on his face as he squeezed the shoulders of the women sitting on either side of him. He leaned in to whisper something in one of their ears, and the girl giggled, swatting him playfully.

"That's him," Maximus growled.

"Dante." I breathed out the name as heat coiled in my stomach. My dragon awoke, hungry and ready to burn the place to the ground.

Maximus took the lead, throwing back the velvet

rope and stepping up onto the platform. "Dante," he growled.

Dante glanced up, his eyebrows furrowed in confusion. "Do I know you?"

"We go way back." Maximus walked around the center table and glared at the two girls until they stood up.

I approached from the other side, and as soon as the girls had vacated their seats, we boxed Dante in. "We haven't had the pleasure," I said. "The name is Cash, and you have something that belongs to us."

Dante looked between us with narrowed eyes. I could see the sweat beading on his forehead and hear the clearing of his throat he tried to hide. We were making the pit master nervous.

"And what might that be?" he asked carefully.

"Ariana," Maximus said. He settled an arm on the back of the couch, leaning close to Dante until the warlock was forced to scoot away. "Where is she?"

"The wolf shifter?" Understanding dawned on him, and he sat bolt upright. "You're the fucking wolf that got my pit shut down!"

Maximus grabbed the back of Dante's neck and squeezed until the little man yelped. "That's right," Maximus said, his voice hard and cold. "Now tell me where she is, and I'll make your death painless."

Dante growled and began raising his hand. Before he could get off a spell, Maximus squeezed his neck again, and the magic licking the air blinked out. "What do you want with her?" Dante squeaked.

I couldn't take it anymore. I grabbed Dante's knee and let my fire burn hot. He ground his teeth as my palm burned through his trousers and then his skin. The smell of burning flesh filled the air, acrid and disgusting. My stomach rolled, but I forced the nausea down. "Don't play games with us. Where is she?"

Dante whined in pain, shifting to try and get away from us both. "I don't have her."

I glanced up to meet Maximus's gaze. He looked ready to commit murder.

"How can we believe you?" he asked Dante.

"I haven't seen her since you took her!" Dante snapped.

"And what about the man you sent to my territory to retrieve her?" Maximus growled.

"I wanted her back for my new show," Dante said. "But then I found the mountain lion. She's brilliant. Far superior to that skinny she-wolf."

My hand burned hotter.

If Maximus hadn't grabbed Dante's throat, his scream would have turned every pair of eyes in the room on us. "You will release every last shifter you have, or we'll be back."

"And you won't get away next time," I threatened.

Dante gulped and nodded. Maximus waited a moment until I pulled my hand back before he released Dante as well. We stood at the same time, while Dante doubled over gripping his seared knee.

I gave the warlock one last glare before slipping out of the VIP area. "We can't just leave these people here." I shot a loaded glance at Maximus as we headed for the stairs.

"We won't," Maximus said. "We'll give Dante a chance to do what's right while we find Ariana."

I nodded in agreement. We climbed the steps back into The Black Sparrow and left the club as quickly as we could. Only when we were back in my car could I breathe again.

"We should see how Owen and Jett fared," I said, yanking my cell phone from my pocket.

"Good idea," Maximus said, slumping back against the seat and rubbing his temple. The hopelessness in his voice twisted in my chest, and again, I felt a kinship with this wolf who I'd spent most of the last decade needling at every opportunity. Maybe I should cut him some slack.

But now wasn't the time to work out our differences. Heart racing, I dialed Owen's number. As I held the phone to my ear and listened to it ring, I could only hope they'd found our mate, and she was safe.

6

OWEN

"That's vampire HQ?" I asked, leaning forward to gaze out the windshield at the huge skyscraper before us. I couldn't believe how tall the building was. How were we supposed to find Ariana inside? It would take days if we couldn't find her by scent.

"Yeah," Jett said. "That's it."

I glanced at the panther alpha. He'd been acting odd since I picked him up. I didn't know Jett well enough to know what might be bothering him, so I had to assume it was worry over Ariana. He hadn't accepted her as a mate like the rest of us, but that didn't mean he wasn't concerned. If nothing else, she was the Silver Shifter, the one who was supposed to bring our clans unity. That benefited Jett's panthers as much as the rest of our clans.

I looked back out the window, craning my neck

to see the top of the building jutting into the night sky high above the city. "How do we get inside?" I asked.

Jett sighed. "Well, we can't just waltz through the front door, so maybe the back."

I shook my head at his smartass reply.

I started up the car—a black, nondescript sedan my family didn't get much use out of anymore. My truck would always be my preferred mode of transportation, but it stuck out on the streets of New York.

I pulled into traffic, and we cut around the back of the building, parking a block away before we slipped into a nearby alleyway.

"You really think the vamps have Ariana?" Jett asked.

I shrugged. "If they don't, then Dante has to. Since we haven't heard from Cash or Maximus yet, I'm assuming they haven't found her."

Jett grunted something that sounded like an agreement, and that was that. We stayed silent as we slipped through the alley and across the street to the back of vampire headquarters. My nostrils flared as we drew closer. I expanded my senses, searching for Ariana's jasmine scent, but all I came up with was blood and ash. The entire area smelled like bloodsuckers and their food. It was disgusting.

"There it is." Jett pointed at a plain gray door with a metal handle.

I tried the handle. Locked.

Jett rolled his eyes. "You think they'd just leave it open?"

I shrugged and broke the handle. It snapped beneath my iron grip, and I tore the door open before motioning Jett inside. "After you."

Though outside the building was a marvel of glass and metal, the interior was concrete and linoleum—or at least the back hallway was.

"What's your plan?" Jett asked. He hadn't been in my valley when we discussed this, so I'd met him in the city.

Now, I paused midstep. Honestly, I didn't have a plan besides tearing apart the building until I found our mate. There was no precedent for this, no real way to plan for the worst thing in the world coming to pass.

"We go floor by floor," I said after a moment of thought. "We stick our heads into every floor and try to catch Ariana's scent. If we can't find her ourselves, we'll head to the penthouse."

"You really want to find out who's running New York since Ariana killed their king?" Jett scoffed.

"It'll be worth it if we find her."

"We'll be lucky to get out alive," Jett countered.

I sighed and levelled a glare at the panther. "If they killed us, it'd mean war. They may be vampires, but they aren't *that* stupid."

Jett met my look with one of his own. I think I was testing his patience. "What about all the vampire attacks lately makes you think the vampires care about going to war with the clans? They might as well have sent a notarized letter saying *I don't give a fuck*."

I hated to admit it, but he had a point. "Let's just hope whoever is in charge knows the Silver Shifter is valuable enough to keep her alive." I stormed down the hall towards a door with the number one painted on it.

Jett rushed to catch up with me. "You're serious?"

"Am I laughing?" Whatever it took, we were getting our mate back. Even if Jett didn't accept Ariana as his mate, I'd seen the way he looked at her—like she might be his salvation or his destruction, he didn't know which. I hoped he'd pull his head out of his ass long enough to find out.

As soon as we reached the door, I knew we'd found what we were looking for. Through a small window I could just make out a set of stairs. I pushed through and stopped at a sign on the wall with a map of the building and its fire exits. We had about fifty floors to go before we reached the penthouse.

"You've got to be fucking kidding me," Jett snarled.

"I hope you're ready to get your cardio in." I flashed him a grimace and started up the first few steps with a hand on the railing until we reached the second floor. Jett followed, his grumbles echoing in the stairwell.

Once we reached the door to floor two, I poked my

head in, took a deep breath and then shut the door. "No sign of our Ana."

Jett didn't so much as grunt in response as I led the way up to the next floor, and the next, and then the next. Soon, I was soaked in sweat, but neither of us complained. I was sure Jett was worried, too, whether he was in denial or not.

Forty-nine floors later, there was still no sign of Ariana.

"One. More. Flight," I panted.

"About fucking time," Jett said.

We climbed the last set of stairs to an iron door with a heavy keypad beside it. My eyebrows furrowed as I inspected it, finding a handprint scanner. Before I could get a good look at it, I caught a flash of red through the small window in the right side of the door.

I peered through the glass to find a lavish room with a dark wood floor and burgundy drapes hanging from every available surface. The decor might have been nice if not for the bodies covered in blood, writhing on top of it.

"Shit," Jett breathed.

"Is that what I think it is?" I asked.

"Blood orgy?"

"Blood orgy."

Nausea turned my stomach as I watched vampires feed on humans, blood pouring down the naked breasts of a woman who might have once had blonde hair, but was now stained red.

"We shouldn't be here," Jett said.

"They might have Ariana," I argued.

"And Ariana is worth both of our lives?" Jett hissed.

"Without a doubt." My hands fisted at my sides. I wanted so badly to break open the door and step inside, demanding they tell me where they'd taken our mate. But if I did that, we could both be dead in minutes. No, we had to play this smart and wait until the party was over. We could hide in the stairwell for a few hours and come back when the room was clear.

Jett grumbled as I watched through the window for a few more moments. When I couldn't take it anymore, I looked away. At least I couldn't smell all the blood. Whatever this door was made of, it was doing a great job of keeping the vampire reak inside.

The squeal of another door opening somewhere below made us both jump. We exchanged a desperate glance before turning back toward the stairwell below. If someone came up, there was nowhere to hide. We had to hope they were going down.

Jett slapped my arm, the sound like a bomb going off in the deadly quiet. I glared at the shifter, but he motioned at the window in the door.

I followed his gaze to find every head in the penthouse had swivelled in our direction. *Shit.* The vampires knew we were here.

"Run," Jett barked.

A whoosh of air brushed my skin, and before we could move, we were surrounded by vampires.

"Run? Why ever would you do such a thing?" A woman with black hair and a high voice grinned at the two of us. "Mistress wants to see you." She slapped a hand down on the keypad, and after a quick scan, the seal on the door opened with a whoosh of air.

The smell of copper filled my nose and mouth. Two vampires pushed us through the door, and I barely kept my balance on the slippery floor inside.

The feeding vampires glared at us, hissing and spitting. I tried to stay calm and hold back the nausea as I was pushed further into the room. I hadn't noticed it before, but at the back of the long room, which may have once been a dining room if the blood-filled cups and discarded cutlery were any clue, stood a platform with a gilded throne. There sat a strikingly beautiful woman with curly blonde hair, ivory skin, and bright blue eyes.

Confusion stopped me short. Vampires had red eyes, not blue. But judging by the woman draped across her lap and the blood-soaked arm against her mouth, that's what she had to be. Only a select few demons drank blood, and vampires didn't associate with them.

My eyes widened, and my heart stuttered a beat as I realized who I was gazing upon.

"The Lamia Queen," Jett said on an exhale.

The queen of all the vampires in the entire world

sat before us, a curious look in her eyes and blood on her lips. Slowly, she lowered the arm of her victim from her mouth and licked her lips.

"Who dares to interrupt my feeding?" she asked. Her voice boomed with power, something I'd never encountered in a vampire before. Though she looked no more than twenty-five, I could see her age in her eyes. The Lamia Queen was *old*. One of the oldest vampires currently in existence and probably the most powerful, she had the power of both vampires and witches.

What the hell was she doing in New York?

"These two shifters, My Lady—" The black-haired vampire pushed us forward before dipping into a curtsy. "—were skulking in the stairwell."

The vampires behind us grabbed our shoulders and forced us to our knees. I ground my teeth as my mind raced to come up with a plan. Surely the Lamia Queen wouldn't kill us. She was the head of the council for the Society of Supernaturals. There were laws she had to abide by.

"You're alphas," the Lamia Queen said, her eyes moving between Jett and me. "Of the New York Clans?"

I exchanged a worried look with Jett. How did she know that just by looking at us?

"Speak," she commanded, raising her chin.

"Jett," my companion said. He raised his chin right back at the queen. "Alpha of the New York panthers."

"I see." The queen's gaze shifted to me. "And you?"

"Owen, Alpha of the New York bears."

The queen's smile twisted and grew. "Two alphas in my house. What an *honor*."

The vampires around us tittered at her obvious sarcasm.

"We're only here to ask you one question, and then we'll get out of your hair," I said.

The queen frowned at the same time the vampire behind me swatted my head. "You will address her majesty properly."

"Your Majesty," I corrected, shifting my weight on my knees.

"Call me Helena," the queen said. She rose to her feet, sending the human on her lap toppling to the floor. Helena stepped over the motionless body to come closer to us. "You have me curious, alphas. What question could you possibly have to ask me?"

She stopped in front of me and bent to grasp my chin and stare me in the eye. My skin crawled at the cold of her skin and the monster in her eyes.

"We're looking for the Silver Shifter," Jett said. "We know you have her."

Helena raised a perfect blonde eyebrow as she shifted her steely gaze from me to Jett. "The Silver Shifter?" Amusement flickered in her eyes. "You've lost your precious gift from the gods? Tsk, tsk."

The queen stood, her black skirt swishing around

her. She turned on her heel and strolled back to her throne.

"Do you have her?" I demanded. My bear strained to the surface suddenly. He recognized a taunt when he saw one. Helena was playing with us. She'd deliberately avoided Jett's question.

Helena paused. "Why on earth do you think I'd snatch up the little wolf and leave her—the cure for vampirism—alive?"

That's when I saw red. A growl ripped from my throat, deep like thunder. It rumbled through the space, silencing the laughing vampires and forcing Helena to look back at me. "You dare threaten our mate?"

"*Our* mate?" Helena's eyes twinkled deviously. "Oh, so the little wolf has both of you wrapped around her little finger. Or is there more? I can't imagine the wolf alpha would let you steal his mate from him."

Well, fuck. I shouldn't have told the Lamia Queen anything. We were here to get information, not give it.

"Just tell us. Do you have her or not?" Jett snapped.

I knew I needed to calm down, but with my Ana's life at stake, it was getting harder and harder not to tear out of my skin and into my bear.

Helena scoffed. "My question remains asked and unanswered. Why—*if* I had your wolf—would I leave her alive? She could be the end of my people. If a person existed who could destroy your people with only her blood, would you leave her breathing?"

"Listen up Queen Bitch, just let us get out of here," Jett snarled.

Helena flashed before us in the blink of an eye. A slap echoed in the space. Before I could follow her movements, she was a few feet away again and Jett's cheek was turning red. "You will speak to me properly, or I will throw you off my balcony, kitten. Is that clear?"

Jett set his jaw and said nothing.

"Your Majesty," I said. I had to get myself and this situation under control, or we were both dead. "Forgive Jett. He's never been one for small talk."

Helena nodded, a small smile returning to her lips. "If I was interested in men, you'd be welcome in my court. Unfortunately, I've had enough of this for one night. You're free to leave. Go on and find your mate."

From the glint in her eyes, she *wanted* us to find Ariana. We were free to leave and lead her straight to our mate, so she could steal her out from under us and destroy every trace of a cure for vampirism.

But that meant...

"You don't have her," I said under my breath.

Helena's eyebrow twitched, and her eyes flashed with barely leashed fury. "Remove them from my sight."

The vampires behind us manhandled us to our feet and through the penthouse to the elevator. After a very quiet ride to the ground, we were escorted out onto the street. Once our guard returned to the building, I grabbed Jett's arm, excitement thrumming through my veins.

"They don't have her," I said.

Jett jerked from my grip and gave me a look like his own personal stormcloud was forming. "I gotta go."

I skidded to a halt. "What?"

"I've got shit to do. If Ariana isn't here, then I'm sure Cash and Maximus found her. I can't wait around all night for their call." Jett shoved his hands in his pockets and took a step back.

"Jett, you can't disappear on us now. Ariana needs you."

Jett scoffed. "I can do whatever the hell I want, Owen. I'm not part of Ariana's little harem."

I narrowed my eyes, but before I could argue further, my phone rang. I pulled it out and checked the caller. Cash.

My heart raced with hope. Maybe they'd found Ariana.

I looked up to share my excitement with Jett, but he was gone. Damn panthers and their gift for disappearing from sight.

Wiping my palm on my jeans, I answered the call, my heart racing. "Did you find her?"

7

JETT

Only when I slid into the back seat of the taxi did I relax. Going through that had been agony, and not just because I'd never wanted to meet the Lamia Queen in my lifetime if I could help it. Now that I was out of the vampire head-quarters, I could breathe a little easier. I could have fought traffic in my own car, but taxis were the more inconspicuous mode of transport. Cash might like to flash his wealth, but I preferred the anonymity of taxis.

I pulled out my phone and texted ahead, muttering my destination to the cab driver as I did. By now, Owen would be on his way to the join the other alphas and discuss their plan. They'd probably have a thing or two to say about my behavior, too. I needed to pull it together, stop acting so erratic. If I wasn't care-ful, they'd catch on to what I had going. Knowing me as well as he did, Cash should have already figured it out, but as usual, he was too busy lusting after a piece of ass to look around him.

I wondered what Owen would have to say to the others when he got back. They'd probably be on the phone to me in minutes, demanding to know why I didn't want to find the Silver Shifter as much as they did. If only they knew. I wanted to make sure she was okay every bit as much as they did—probably more. But she wasn't my mate. Despite my sister's insistence to the contrary, I didn't need a mate.

The others apparently didn't share my opinion. I could still feel the waves of agitation that had been rolling off Owen the whole time we'd been in Vamp HQ, and it wasn't just about being surrounded by bloodsuckers. He was hurting for his mate so bad it almost made me hurt with him. I didn't know Owen well, but I could tell that out of the four clan alphas, he was the best of us. Ask anyone else, and they'd probably say I was the worst. After some of the things I'd done lately, I was beginning to think they'd be right.

I hated lying to Owen, but I didn't have much choice. It seemed that more and more lately, I hadn't had much choice about the things I'd had to do. When I did have a choice, the options were between shitty and shittier.

I pointed to the non-descript warehouse building, and the taxi coasted through the nearly deserted parking lot to the guard station beside the gate before rocking to a halt.

"What is this place?" the cabbie asked, looking more than a little freaked when he saw the semi-automatic rifle pointed at us.

"Nowhere," I said, handing him the cab fare. I slid out of the car and slammed the door before he could ask more questions. I waved for him to go, and after a second, he sped off. I turned to the guard, holding up both hands. "It's just me. Jett."

"Proof of identity," the guard barked, keeping his weapon trained on me.

I stopped at the key pad near the gate, far enough from the guard station that he could shoot me if I got any ideas. He looked a little jumpy even though his little booth had all kinds of protection spells on it. Humans had no idea of everything supernaturals could do, and I didn't blame them for taking precautions.

Instead of punching in a number or scanning my handprint, I slipped on the black and silver device that looked a little like a pair of high-tech headphones. An imposter could steal a pin number or copy everything about a person, down to their fingerprints and retinas. But no one with that kind of magic could fake the brainwaves of a shifter.

I hit the 'on' switch and waited for the doctors to give my brain the stamp of approval.

"See anything you like?" I asked after a minute, knowing they'd hear me through the headset.

"You look agitated," came the answer.

"I'm fine," I said. "You can read my brainwaves, Doc, not my mind."

I replaced the headset and saluted the guard, who hit a switch to unlock the gate. I walked through and slid my wallet out, inserted my keycard, and waited for the locks to disengage. Two cameras pointed at me from above the door, but I kept my eyes focused straight ahead. The doc had already seen too much of my excitement. I didn't want to give her any more ammunition. When I heard the click of the locks, I turned the knob and entered the low, metal building.

The moment I stepped inside, I was surrounded by bright, fluorescent lights, polished linoleum floors, and industrial ceilings. Outside, it might look like a warehouse, but inside, it looked like a hospital. I knew appearances were deceiving on both counts.

I started down the corridor, moving faster than I should. I didn't want to get caught up in theorizing and guessing before I saw her.

"Jett," called a voice from down a side hall.

Ignoring it, I hurried toward the observation room.

"Jett," the voice called again. The doctor was beside me in moments, clinging to my elbow like a leech.

I reminded myself that she was one of the good

guys. We were on the same side—the side that hated vampires.

"Someone's in a hurry," Dr. Siegfred said, eyeing me.

"I want to see the patient, that's all," I said. "I can't wait to hear about your progress."

When she showed no signs of leaving my side, I decided to let her follow me. I wasn't going to be stopped until my eyes were on the prize.

"You should really hear what I have to say before you go barging in there," the doctor said as I reached the door to the observation room.

Ignoring her, I turned the knob and entered the long, rectangular room with a wall made of glass. It overlooked a large room with a bed and various machines and pieces of medical equipment. My chest squeezed when I caught sight of the slight figure strapped to the bed, the tell-tale silver hair strewn across the pillow. Unaware that she was being watched, she twisted her head from side to side, then tried to sit, straining against her restraints.

"She has been a less-than-ideal participant," Muriel said, tapping her clipboard. "We've tried to give her more freedom, rewarding her for good behavior, but she's shown us very little cooperation even when we explained we are working to eradicate the vampire threat."

I barely heard her. My eyes stayed riveted on the

woman in the bed, her gaze flying to the clock and her struggles intensifying.

I choked on a breath, trying to control my panther, who had suddenly risen up in mutinous fury, screeching to be free and go to the woman he thought was his mate. From the moment we'd laid eyes on her, he'd claimed her as his own, but it hadn't stopped me from betraying her.

I was more than an animal, though. My human side was rational and could think beyond myself. This was for the greater good—a necessity, in fact. When vampires ceased to exist, the rest of the world could relax. Only then would it be safe for us to take mates and have children. Only then could we be sure that we'd live to see our children grow into their roles and have families of their own.

"We've been extracting a sample of her blood each day," Muriel said. "It would help if we had her cooperation. We were hoping you'd talk to her, and—"

"Me?" I asked incredulously. "Why would she listen to me?

"Well, we assumed you knew her personally," she said, eyeing me suspiciously. "You did turn her over to us."

It sounded so much worse when she put it like that. It was true, though. As much as I hated to admit it, I deserved every bit of Ariana's wrath.

"Sorry to break it to you, Doc, but Ariana hates

me," I said. "And I never had her in my possession, so I couldn't have turned her over to you."

"You told us where and how to find her," Dr. Siegfred continued, leveling me with a gaze that was both exasperated and curious. She was obviously dying to know the complexities of our relationship, but I wasn't about to get into that with her. I hadn't even gotten into it with my sister yet.

"If you need someone to sweet talk her, sorry, but I won't be of any help to you," I said.

"Well, if we can't get her to talk, we'll just have to do it the hard way," she said. "It may take longer, but with enough blood tests, we'll figure out everything she could tell us and then some. We need to isolate the components of her blood that are curing vampires. If we knew why her blood could do this, it might make the process go more quickly, but in the end, we'll get there either way."

I didn't like the sound of that. My ears were ringing with a panther scream that only I could hear, but I held tight to my control, not letting him bully me into submission. He might not see it with his primitive brain, but I could see it. Ariana wasn't our mate. She was our savior. She was going to make sure no more panthers grew up without fathers because of blood-sucking parasites.

"What she's essentially doing is bringing them back to life," Dr. Siegfred was saying. "Not killing them but turning them from monsters into ordinary humans. It's extraordinary, really. We were hoping you could frame the question in such a way that she sees that she's the solution. It benefits all shifters—all four clans. That's a Silver Shifter's job, isn't it? We hoped she'd be an enthusiastic participant. I can't imagine what shifter wouldn't be, especially after what they've done to her."

"You're not hurting her, are you?" I asked, stalking up and down the small room, my arms crossed tightly over my chest, keeping myself contained.

"Of course not," Muriel said. "We're just keeping her subdued until we can determine the specific properties that make the transformation of vampires possible, so we can manufacture these aspects and not rely on an unwilling subject."

"I'll do my best," I said, my heart wrenching at the sight of the scared girl twisting in the bed below. I didn't think she'd listen to a single word I had to say, but I had to at least try. So much depended on this girl. Everything depended on her.

"We are as determined as you, Jett," Muriel said. "We want to form an alliance that is mutually beneficial to humans and shifters. To make the world safe for all of us."

The only way to do that was to eradicate vampires, and the only way to do *that* was to use the Silver Shifter's gift. I kept telling myself that as the door to Ariana's room opened and a nurse entered. Ariana began to snarl, her eyes wide with terror. I squeezed my hands into fists, my claws extending and piercing the flesh of my palms. My teeth extended as well, and I barely held myself back from leaping through the glass window.

My panther didn't give a shit about isolating components and manufacturing aspects, about persuasive arguments or even uniting the clans. He just wanted to go to his mate, to free her and protect her from anyone who meant her harm—even me.

8

ARIANA

As the poison slowly seeped from the syringe into my vein, I felt my strength draining away. They didn't just take my blood to make me weak. They gave me something, something that cooled the heat of my dragon and put her to sleep, so I couldn't even hear her inside me.

My wolf, however, made up for the silence. The silver put us into a state of constant pain that dulled my mind and left her crying for relief. I wanted to rip them to shreds with my bare, human hands for hurting my wolf that way. They had no idea. No idea what it was like to live with this creature inside me, to be trusted to care for her and keep her safe, and to fail her so miserably. They didn't have to hear her incessant, piteous whimpering, and know that they were once again powerless to protect her.

And they had no idea what it was doing to me.

Something inside me was growing in my lucid moments, like a rumbling of thunder in the distance, growing every day. When I unleashed it...

I was going to fucking kill each and every one them, ruthlessly and methodically. I just had to find some way...

As the silver seeped into me, even my resolve weakened. I sank back on the bed, the icy burn of the injection racing up my arm, through my veins. My eyes fluttered closed as the ice invaded my mind, filling it with a dull throbbing and swirling, confused thoughts.

Maybe if I cooperated they would stop injecting poison into my veins, or whatever they were putting in me to subdue my dragon. Maybe they would stop spraying silver down my throat. I shivered under the thin blankets, wanting to curl up, to hold my middle and offer my wolf whatever solace she took from my human company. But my arms and legs were strapped to the bed, keeping me from offering even that small comfort.

I closed my eyes. When I opened them, I heard a shout in the hallway. The door blinked open like an eye, and suddenly, one of my mates stood over me.

No, not one of my mates.

Jett.

I knew I must be dreaming. Jett wouldn't visit me in the hospital.

"Ariana."

My eyes snapped open. He was still there. He leaned over the bed, bracing one hand on each edge, his face close to mine. For a second, I could only stare into his black velvet eyes. My wolf whined pitifully, trying to connect with her mate, thinking he was here to rescue us.

But this wasn't a hospital where I'd been taken to heal. Jett might not visit me in one of those, but apparently, he'd visit me in the kind of hospital that strapped you to a bed and tortured your inner animal.

I nudged my wolf down, knowing that once again, she'd be disappointed by a human. This time it wasn't me, though. As the realization of what this meant sank in, my lips pulled back from my teeth even though my wolf was too weak to come out and fight.

"Jett," I growled, a voice coming out of me that I didn't think I'd ever heard. It was laced with pain that bordered on hatred.

A tiny smile tugged the corner of Jett's full lips, but it never reached his eyes. "A pleasure, as always," he said, straightening.

"You did this?" I demanded, straining against my restraints. "I knew it was you. All that time, I thought you were colluding with the vampires. But this... This is worse." A growl rumbled somewhere inside me, and Jett took a step back, looking uncertain. Even I didn't know where it was coming from—this strength that fueled my anger. My dragon slept, and my wolf was poisoned by silver and beyond fighting. Something fanned my anger, though, pushing up inside me like a building tidal wave.

"Come on, Quicksilver," Jett said, his eyes almost pleading. "You don't mean that."

"Don't fucking tell me what I mean," I said through gritted teeth.

Jett held up both hands. "Okay, fine. You meant it. And I don't blame you. This isn't what I had in mind when they told me what they wanted."

"Who?" I asked.

"Dr. Siegfred," he said. "The HCA."

"What does it matter who it is?" I asked. "It could be Dante keeping me in a cage and forcing me to fight, or vampires keeping me locked away so no one can use me against them, or these assholes. They're all the same to me."

"You've got it all wrong," Jett said. "The HCA is the opposite of vampires. They want to help people, not hurt them."

"And yet, they treat me like a prisoner, someone less than human. It makes no difference to me what kind of monster captures me. They're all monsters."

Jett's lips tightened, and his eyes cut away from mine. "I'll have them untie you," he muttered.

"That's all you have to say?" I asked, nearly choking on incredulousness.

"No," he said, his jaw tensing. "They shouldn't have kept you like this, but what they're doing isn't wrong, Ariana. They're ridding the world of a plague. Maybe they didn't go about it the right way, but from what I hear, you didn't give them much choice."

I blinked at him, my hands fisting, anger thudding in my temples. "Are you fucking delusional, Jett? You think I gave them no choice but to attack me repeatedly, to follow me to my mate's territory, break into the house in the middle of the night, and kidnap me? But I guess you're going to tell me that was all for my own good. I gave them no choice but to kidnap me, drug me, poison me, and chain me to a bed, after all."

Jett sighed and ran a hand down his face. "You're making this difficult, Ariana. All we want is to stop a group of mass murderers from killing. Yes, it's unfortunate, but right now you're the only thing we have that can stop them."

"And you didn't think to just come to me and ask?" I growled.

"Don't you want to stop them?" Jett asked. "How can you defend vampires? Haven't they taken everything from you, too?"

Our eyes caught, and for a long moment, neither of us spoke. My mind caught on that last word.

Of course this was personal. That's why Jett was so determined, why he'd betray the other clans, risking his life and a war that could wipe out his entire clan. To him, it was worth it to wipe out the vampires. What could make him hate them so much he'd sacrifice everything to erase them?

It wasn't just a dislike of bloodsuckers, the enemy

of shifters by their very nature. This was something else.

"Vampires didn't take everything from me," I said slowly. "They tried, on that roof. But most of my life, it was warlocks who owned me, who made me fight. Vampires were nothing but their henchmen in the pits."

Jett's jaw clenched, but he didn't speak.

"But they took everything from you," I said. "That's it, right? That's what would make you betray all four clans. So who did they take?"

"No one," Jett said, his eyes fixed on the wall beyond my bed.

"You wouldn't betray your own people for no one," I said. "You're not only betraying them, though, Jett. You're betraying your mate, and worse than that, your panther."

His eyes finally snapped back to mine, fury flashing there. "You're not my mate," he growled. "I have no mate. I can't risk forming a mate bond when at any time, the vampires could come in and take her from me—or me from her."

My eyes narrowed. I had already learned that my mates had lived very different lives from mine, but I didn't know much about Jett's life at all. I knew wolves usually only had one mate—at least they had until me. But maybe panthers had more. "They took your mate?" I asked.

An unexpected pain formed in my chest, not at the

thought of Jett having another mate but at the thought of anyone hurting him that way. Even after he'd done this to me, he was still a person, and a person in pain would always tug at my heart. Too bad it didn't go both ways.

"Not my mate," Jett said. "My father."

"What happened?" I whispered, wanting to reach for his hand but unable. My own hands were still bound.

"They took him, that's what happened," Jett said, crossing his arms over his chest. "They kidnapped him and held him for ransom, demanding that we cooperate with them in attacking the other clans. They knew his successor wasn't ready to take over or make decisions like that, and they thought we'd give in right away."

"And you didn't?" I whispered.

Jett sank onto the bed at my feet, his back to me and his shoulders slumped. "No," he said. "I let Cash convince me..." He paused, then shook his head. "No, *I* chose not to negotiate with them. Cash and I went after them, but we were too late. They found out we were coming for them, and they killed him."

"I'm sorry," I said, barely able to swallow.

Jett stiffened. "I know you want to see the best in everyone, Quicksilver, but there are no good vampires."

"You can't know that," I said. "They might think the same about shifters."

He stood and turned to face me. "And if they had the chance, do you really think they'd hesitate to kill every single one of us, starting with you?"

"I think that if you're going to eradicate an entire species using an unwilling weapon to do it, they might not be the bad guys."

Jett's brows lowered, his eyes darkening. "What are you saying?"

"They're not the monsters here, Jett," I said. "You are."

9

MAXIMUS

I tapped my fingers against the cold glass of beer in my hand, glancing up at the door every time it swung open. My pulse raced with my fingers, and sweat trickled down my spine. I needed to get it together, but every second I spent without Ariana safe was driving me mad.

"Take a breath, Maximus," Cash said, levelling me a concerned look. "Owen will be here any minute."

"They didn't find Ariana," I said. I watched the condensation drip down my glass and bead on my skin. The cold sent a chill down my spine. We hadn't found Ariana with Dante, and it seemed Owen and Jett hadn't found her with the vampires. Anyone could have her.

The chime on the door went off, and Owen strode inside, his gaze sweeping the bar and finding mine. He nodded a quick greeting before he worked his way through the crowded shifter bar and slid into the booth beside Cash.

"Hey," Cash greeted the bear shifter. "Jett didn't come with you?"

A frown darkened Owen's expression as he rubbed his bearded cheek. "No. He took off right after we were kicked out of vampire headquarters."

"Kicked out?" I raised my eyebrows at the imposing man. He nearly smashed Cash into the wall he took up so much space. I was happy to have him on Ariana's side—and my side, I realized. Between Cash's hot head and my urge to rip apart New York until I found my mate, we might have blown the whole search if not for Owen keeping us steady.

"Yeah," Owen said. "The vamps caught on to us and brought us before..." He broke off, a shudder quaking through his massive frame.

"Before who?" Cash asked.

"The Lamia Queen."

"What?" I barked. My grip tightened convulsively, and glass shards went flying. I hardly felt it as my mind raced to come up with a reason the Queen of Vampires had come to New York. This couldn't be good. The vampires had to be gearing up for something big if their queen was in town. With everything else going on, it couldn't be a coincidence that Ariana had gone missing just as the vamp queen arrived. Could it?

Owen detailed their meeting while a waitress

stopped by with a rag to clean up the glass. I apologized profusely for breaking the glass and dousing the table and floor in beer, but she shrugged it off, saying it happened all the time in a shifter bar.

"And she just let you go?" Cash asked Owen when he finished his story.

"I was suspicious, too," Owen said. "I thought they must be planning to follow us and let us do all the work of finding her. I noticed a tail following from a safe distance on the way here, so it seems I was right."

"Then they don't have her," I realized aloud. "If they had her, why would they send a tail?"

Cash's eyes went wide as the realization hit him.

"Right," Owen rumbled. "They sent a squad of vamps after me, hoping I'd eventually lead them to Ariana."

A growl ripped from my throat. "If the vamps don't have her, then who does?"

Cash and Owen exchanged a look.

"I don't know," Cash admitted. "I'm fairly certain Dante was telling the truth."

"If the vamps don't have her... And Dante doesn't have her... Then where is she?" Owen asked.

That was the question we all wanted answered. As I looked at the other two faces at the table, I realized they were as distraught as I was. At least, I knew Owen was. His cheeks were haggard and his eyes rimmed with dark circles after two days of fruitless searching. I couldn't read Cash as well. He'd had a century to master hiding his emotions. For all I knew, he was responsible for Ariana's disappearance.

I squeezed my eyes shut and buried my face in my hands. Ariana hadn't run away this time, like she had that first day at my house. She had three mates now, three men who would die to find her, three men who she loved. At least, she'd said she loved me. Why hadn't I said it back? What if I never had the chance now?

No. I couldn't think like that. I would tell her when I saw her next. Because there would be a next time. Despite a bit of awkwardness at Owen's place, Ariana had seemed happier than I'd ever seen her. And I was going to spend the rest of my life bringing that happiness into her eyes over and over.

I lifted my head. She had been taken against her will by someone who didn't leave a scent. Who didn't leave a scent? "We should return to the scene of the crime," I said.

Cash's fists curled on top of the table. "You're right. Maybe we missed something."

Owen nodded, hope sparking in his eyes. "Good idea."

"We should call Jett," Cash added. "We need all of us on this one."

I exchanged a wary glance with Owen. From the look in the bear alpha's eyes, he had the same reservations about Jett that I did. But how could we tell Cash, Jett's childhood friend, that we had a feeling

Jett had something to do with our mate's disappearance?

Before either of us could say a word, Cash pulled out his phone and hit a button. The phone rang a few times before Jett's voice came through with a turse, *"What is it?"*

"We're heading back to Bear Clan territory to check out the area where Ari was kidnapped again, see if we missed anything. Whatever you're doing, drop it and meet us there. It can't be as important as our mate," Cash said in a rush of words.

I heard a faint sigh from the other line before Jett's voice came through again.

"I can't," Jett said. "I'm busy. Text me if you need anything."

With that, the line went dead. Cash's eyebrows furrowed as he lowered the phone from his ear. "That was... abrupt," he said.

I grunted an affirmative, not quite ready to share my suspicions with Cash, though the phone call had definitely confirmed some of my fears. Jett was avoiding us. It could be something to do with his clan. Maybe there were panther politics at play that he hadn't shared. But right now, there should be nothing more important than Ariana. She was the Silver Shifter. That was the most pressing clan matter possible. Not to mention that she was his mate, too, even if he refused to claim her.

The thought stopped me up for a second. When

had I started thinking of her as ours, not *mine*? When had I started to believe that even an unclaimed, unco-operative mate was her mate, though he refused to admit it, just because she said so?

Maybe when I'd started to trust Ariana's wolf as much as my own, as a mate should. Maybe when I'd realized I could lose her, it had stopped mattering how many mates she had. That didn't change the love that had grown between us—the love that was going to save her.

A FEW HOURS LATER, we arrived back at Owen's sister's house. We said a quick hello to his sister and her kids before inspecting the kitchen and coming up empty. There was no new smell. No new clue to lead us to Ariana. I had the most sensitive nose for scenting, and even I couldn't find a trace of anything. Jett had defi-nitely not been there.

I trudged out of the back door and went straight for the woods.

"Maximus, we already tried tracking them through the woods," Cash called from the house.

"This is what we're here for, isn't it?" I yelled over my shoulder. If we were going to play detective we had to search the entire area, including the tracks in the woods. It might lead us nowhere, but I had to try. This was the only thing we could do. After this, there were no more options. We'd have exhausted all of our ideas, and Ariana would remain missing.

We had to find something. We *would* find something.

I held onto that thought as I followed the path into the woods. After a minute, the thud of Cash and Owen's footsteps followed, and soon we were walking side by side into the small clearing where tire tracks marred the earth.

Before anyone could stop me, I was stripping off my clothes and tossing them onto a nearby bush.

"What are you doing?" Cash asked.

I barely shot him a look before I reached inside me for my wolf. He was growling and ready to be unleashed, clawing at my skin for freedom. He wanted to find Ariana just as badly as I did.

"I'll inspect the area," I said, my words garbled as I unleashed the beast.

When I blinked, I was on all fours, my senses heightened and the world around me sharp. I shook, my fur rustling slightly as my wolf settled around me.

New smells and sights opened before my eyes. I lowered my nose closer to the ground and breathed in deeply. I could smell the burn of rubber tires and the acrid stench of asphalt stuck in the wheels. There was also the earthy smell of forest and a metallic scent I couldn't quite place.

I did a sweep of the clearing, searching for any clue to Ariana's whereabouts. But besides her sweet rain scent, and that of the vehicle, I couldn't make out the smell of her assailants. I paused near one of the deeper tire tracks, kneading anxiously at the ground with my massive paws.

This wasn't right. How could someone hide their scent so completely? It didn't make any sense.

"Have you found anything, Max?" Owen asked, a hopeful edge to his voice.

A whine crept from my throat before I could stop it. Sadness split Owen's hopeful gaze, and he nodded solemnly.

With nothing else to search, I shifted back and quickly slipped my clothes on. My wolf rumbled inside me, unhappy at being caged so soon. I tried to remember when was the last time I'd shifted for a hunt, or even a run in the woods, but since Ariana appeared in my life, I had been so consumed with taking care of her and protecting her from these attacks that I hadn't had time to care for my wolf properly. I silently promised him a real hunt as soon as we had our mate back.

"Let's follow the tracks," Owen said.

Cash gave Owen a pitying look. He thought Ariana was gone. He thought we'd never find her. I clenched my fists and glared at him. From the way he was acting, maybe he and Jett were both in on it. Turning my back, I followed the tracks in silent fury. I wasn't ready to give up even if Cash was, even if he was responsible for this and didn't want us to find her. I would find her if I had to walk around the entire fucking globe to do it.

My fellow alphas followed in silence until we reached the road. It was a small backwoods highway with only one lane on either side of the road. The pavement was rough and cracked, and several potholes had lost their filling all across the asphalt. I took a deep breath and found the same smell of the tires, along with the metallic scent that was unfamiliar to me.

There was nothing else here. I'd hoped beyond hope that maybe Ariana had had the chance to drop something, or leave us some kind of message. But all hope was lost. My mate was gone.

My wolf howled inside me—a mournful, desolate sound that sent an ache spiraling into my bones. I wanted to curl up and comfort my hurting wolf, to never see the sun again. What was life without my mate? I'd waited so long for her. I'd only found her for a brief moment in time. And now she was gone.

"Owen, where are you going?" Cash shouted.

I looked up to find Owen racing down the side of the highway. My eyebrows furrowed as I watched him go. With every step his speed increased until he was nearly a blur.

"Did he find something?" I asked. My heart pounded hard, daring to hope that maybe not all was lost.

"I don't know," Cash said.

Together we jogged to catch up with the bear alpha until I caught sight of what Owen must have seen. Traffic lights.

Far down the road were a set of traffic lights. They shone green, a beacon of hope that had my legs pumping and my pulse racing. If there were traffic lights, there was a good chance there were also traffic cams. We might be able to figure out who took Ariana yet.

I skidded to a halt next to Owen. He grinned as he motioned at the traffic cameras mounted to the metal polls hoisting the lights over the intersection.

Cash pushed past me and grabbed Owen's face in his hands before planting a kiss on his cheek. "You brilliant bastard!"

Owen stared at the dragon alpha. "Thank... you?"

Hope swelled inside of me until I couldn't help but smile for what felt like the first time in my life. Cash and Owen grinned with me, bouncing excitedly from foot to foot. "We're going to find her," I said.

"Damn right we are," Cash agreed.

"Text that asshole panther," I said. "We need that footage."

Cash nodded, his phone already in hand. He typed out a quick message before we began the trek back to the house. It seemed like it took forever, but with excitement pounding in my veins, I had to stop myself from running the whole way.

The dragon alpha's phone dinged the second we stepped into Owen's kitchen. "He sent it."

I crowded Cash on one side while Owen took the other. We both squeezed in to get a look at the footage Jett had sent us on Cash's small phone screen. Cash hit the play button and after a few minutes of fast forwarding, we found it.

From a distance, we could just make out a van speeding out of the sideroad onto the main highway. It skidded into the far lane before shifting back onto the road and tearing through the intersection. My heart raced as we watched.

"Go back," Owen said.

Cash reversed the clip, then stopped to play it again, and then again. On the third watch, he paused as the van sped through the intersection, giving us a good look at two figures sitting in the front seats in full black military gear.

"The license plate." Owen pointed at it, and I had to restrain myself from yanking the phone out of Cash's hands.

"A friend on the NYC police force owes me a favor," Cash said. He screenshotted the license plate and texted it to his cop friend.

A few seconds later, his phone chimed again.

"He's running the plates now, but it might take a while to get back to us," Cash said.

My skin buzzed with nerves, and I had to squeeze my fists to keep from grabbing something and hurling it in frustration. I was suddenly full of energy, ready to go, and we had to wait. I asked Owen if I could take a quick run in his valley to appease my wolf, though I wouldn't disrespect the bears by hunting on their grounds. A run would comfort my wolf and use some of my energy, calming me and getting me centered for the big challenge. We would get our mate back. I was ready to tear anyone apart who stood in my way. No one could stop me once I'd found her. My mate would be back in my arms soon, and this time, I wouldn't hesitate to tell her exactly how I felt.

10

ARIANA

fter my tirade, Jett left the room without another word. I heard some yelling in the hall that consisted of some very choice words, and a few minutes later, the doctor appeared escorted by two hulking guards.

"It seems you'd be more comfortable if you weren't restrained," Muriel said.

"You think?" I grumbled. I had a moment of feeling grateful that Jett had torn her a new one for chaining me up like a criminal, but it was quickly snuffed out by the reminder that Jett was actually responsible for my being here.

"We may have been overly cautious about our own safety," Muriel said as the guards removed the straps holding my feet. "But the important thing is that you're safe."

Safe, but too weak to do anything but lie on the bed like an invalid.

"So, let me get this straight," I said. "I think I'm getting the whole picture now. Jett told you people about my blood curing those vamps, and you decided I was the magical cure you'd been looking for. Jett had his human henchmen kidnap me so you can experiment on me and try to replicate my blood and wipe out vampires."

"Oh, no," Muriel said. "We don't work for Jett. We're just lucky to have a shifter in agreement with our organization. We were hoping you'd be as cooperative, considering your connection to him."

I narrowed my eyes. Surely he hadn't told her that I was his mate. "What connection?"

"He knew about your blood," she said. "I'm sure that's not something a lot of people know. The vampires aren't going to be telling anyone about it, that's for sure."

"Okay, so Jett's colluding with humans to wipe out vamps," I mused aloud. "And I'm just the pawn. Cool."

For some reason, it almost hurt worse that he'd throw me under the bus for his agenda than because he had a personal vendetta against me. He didn't even care about me enough to hate me. I was just a means to an end to him, a tool to be used for something he'd wanted long before I showed up.

"You just let us know when you're ready to cooperate," Muriel said, flicking her syringe before she jabbed it into me again. "Until then, we've agreed to Jett's demands that you not be restrained. Unfortunately, that means we have to increase your dosage to keep everyone safe."

I bared my teeth at her, feeling my survival instinct kicking in, closing off other thoughts. My mate's betrayal didn't matter. Nothing mattered but living, just as it had in the pits. Then, they had wanted me strong, had made me work for them. Here, they wanted me weak, wanted me to lie here and be passive while they took what they wanted. In the end, no matter how different it was, it boiled down to the same thing. I wasn't my own. I was a prisoner, and I had to survive. That was all that mattered.

When the doctor and her guards left, I was so weak I could barely stand. I made it to the wall where the door always appeared, but all I could do was slide down it and rest. When someone brought dinner, I could barely lift the spoon to my mouth to eat the soup before falling asleep.

The next time I woke, my head felt clearer for a moment. That meant the poison was wearing off, and the nurse was going to return to inject me soon. I sat up, my whole body trembling. Something inside me stirred insistently, pressing up on my consciousness, urging me to fight though I had no energy.

"Morning, Quicksilver," said a deep, drawling voice. I twisted around to see Jett sitting in a chair next to the mirror.

"What are you doing here?" I snarled.

"Nice to see you, too," he said with a smirk.

"Why would it be nice to see you?" I asked. "You're draining the life out of me just like the vampires you hate so much."

Jett rolled his eyes. "Are you going to quote Nietzsche again?"

"Who?"

"Nietzsche," he said, looking at me like I was missing a few brain cells. "You know, the nihilist guy you quoted last night? 'Battle not with monsters, lest ye become a monster.' That guy."

"Sounds pretty smart," I said, shrugging one shoulder. "I don't know him."

Jett shook his head. "That's right. You were raised by vampires. Do you even know how to read?"

"Yes, I know how to read," I snapped. "In case you forgot, my parents didn't die until I was twelve. Maybe you didn't learn to read until after that, but I must be advanced."

Jett grinned. "So, the last book you read must be... What do twelve-year-old girls like to read? *Twilight*? No wonder you think vampires can be redeemed."

"Actually, that's the second time I've heard you mention that book. Seems like it's what *you* like to read." I held up both hands. "No judgment."

"I prefer Friedrich Nietzsche," he said, looking annoyed.

I crossed my arms over my chest and screwed my

lips to one side, studying him. "So, you're well read. Interesting. I didn't peg you as the bookish sort."

"I'm a man of many talents," he said, eyeing me with an appreciative glance that made a completely inappropriate tremor awaken inside me.

"And in all that reading, you never learned not to kidnap a girl and start a war?"

"Start a war?" he asked, glaring.

"Yeah," I said. "Don't you think the other clans are going to be pissed when they find out you kidnapped their mate and poisoned her with silver? You don't actually think you're going to get away with this, do you?"

"We're not going to kill you," Jett said. "I had them untie you, and we're not hurting you. We're going to let you go as soon as we figure out how to artificially replicate what your blood contains. The other clans will be glad to be rid of vampires, too."

"Wow," I said, shaking my head. "I might be a little behind on my reading, but at least I'm not completely delusional."

Jett crossed his arms, his posture mirroring mine, his biceps bulging inside his purple T-shirt. "I can't decide if I like you better when you're insulting me or begging me to mate with you."

My mouth dropped open in indignation. Finally I spluttered, "I never begged."

"That's right," Jett said, flashing his white teeth in a grin. "You ordered me to mate with you."

"I didn't order, beg, or demand anything," I said through gritted teeth. "I told you that you were my mate. Obviously, that's not going to happen after this. Even if you were the only mate I'd ever get, and I didn't have the other three, I'd never be able to trust you again."

Jett's lips pinched together, and he rocked back on his heels, staring at the wall above my head.

"You can't even look at me," I said. "You should feel guilty. And guess what, Jett? I do have the other three. They're going to find me, and they're going to get me out of here. And when they try to make you pay for what you did, I'm going to stop them."

Jett's gaze snapped back to mine, his eyebrows raised in surprise.

"That's right," I said. "They're going to want to kill you for this, but I'm going to forgive you. It'll be enough for me to know that I have three mates who love me. The only companion you'll have for the rest of your life is regret."

Jett's eyes hardened. "You're being unreasonable," he said. "All we're asking is for your cooperation. When the vampires are gone, you'll see that it was worth it."

"If you were asking for my cooperation, I'd have a choice," I said. "I could refuse, and you'd respect that. This isn't asking, Jett. It's taking what you want, whether I agree to it or not. It's turning vampires human, whether they agree to it or not. Maybe they like being vampires as much as we like being shifters. How would you like it if someone took away your panther?"

Jett's nostrils flared, and he glared at me. "I can see we're not going to get anywhere this morning," he said. "I'll visit later. Hopefully you'll have come to your senses by then, and you'll see that this is the only way shifters are ever going to find peace. I don't know how you haven't figured that out in the past two weeks. The vampires will never stop attacking until you're dead, Ariana. They'll never let you live now that they know what you can do. You're a biological weapon to their people. Either we take them out, or they take you out. There's only one choice you need to make here—you or them?"

"*You've reached Jett. Leave a message.*"

I growled and slammed the end call button on my phone. I must have called the panther alpha a hundred times, but he was still avoiding us. Unease crept through me, swelling into a ball of dread in the pit of my stomach. I saw the way Maximus and Owen exchanged a suspicious look every time Jett didn't answer. I saw the flash of suspicion in their eyes, but I couldn't relate it to the man I'd grown up with. Jett and I might not be as close as we once were, but I still liked to think of us as friends. A friend wouldn't betray me.

Closing my eyes, I took a deep breath before opening them again. I looked to the dark night sky twinkling with stars. You didn't get this kind of view in the city.

"No answer?" Maximus asked.

I sighed. "No."

I didn't need to turn around to know that the alphas were once again exchanging a glance. They thought Jett was up to no good, and I was starting to agree with them. It had been hours since Jett answered his phone. Either something had happened to him, or he was up to something.

I hoped it was the former, despite the fact that meant he'd be in trouble.

"I'm going to try Cassandra," I said. I flipped open my contact list and scrolled until I found Jett's sister. Though she was a few years younger than Jett, she'd always followed Jett and I around when we were friends. He'd been just a teenager, and I'd been...somewhere around that in dragon years. Jett had always tried to ditch his sister, yelling at her to leave us alone, but I didn't mind her. Who cared if his little sister followed us into the woods while I stretched my wings and Jett his paws?

"Good idea," Owen said. "Maybe she's heard from him."

I hit the number for Jett's second, held the phone to my ear, and listened to the buzz for only half a second before she picked up.

"Hello? Jett, is that you?" Cassandra asked. Her voice was high with desperation, pulling on my heart-strings.

"You didn't save my number? I'm hurt," I said, a smirk tugging at my lips. In truth, she probably hated me worse than Jett. After his father's death, Jett had blamed me, and he'd cut ties. Of course that meant I hadn't spoken to Cassandra since then. She'd grown from a pesky sister following her brother around to a powerful, well-respected Second-in-Command in that time, but she would always be little Cassie to me. To her, I'd probably always be the jerk who had made her brother want to ditch her and hang out with a cool, older dragon. Not to mention she might blame me just as Jett did. After all, I had been much older and more experienced than Jett, and I'd given him the advice that was best for his clan--and worst for his family. At the time, I'd thought I was doing the right thing. I'd done what my own parents would have wanted me to do in that situation. Only later had I realized that Jett's relationship with his father was world's away from the one I had with my father. There was no right answer in that situation. Either way, something horrible would have happened. Either way, Jett would have needed someone to blame, and I was the easy choice.

"It is you," Cassandra said, interrupting my bitter thoughts. "Damn, I haven't heard that accent in awhile. How've you been?"

My eye twitched involuntarily. "I've been better," I said. I didn't want to lie to Jett's sister, but I couldn't convey my suspicions to her, either. "Listen, I can't explain everything right now, but have you heard from that troublesome brother of yours?"

A weighted silence remained on the line for

several long moments, making nervous sweat dampen my palms.

"Cassandra?" I asked.

"I'm here. Sorry." Again, she paused. "I was hoping you called because you'd heard from Jett. I haven't seen or heard from him in two days."

"That's not like him," I said. He and Cassandra were close from what I understood of their lives now.

"Right?" Cassandra sighed. "If you hear from him, tell him to call me. We need him right now."

Curiosity got the better of me. "Is something wrong with the panthers?"

"You know I can't tell you that, Cash. Don't even ask."

Damn. "Well, at least I tried."

Cassandra laughed half-heartedly. "Seriously, though. We need him. If you hear from him, tell him Cassie said to get his narrow ass home."

I smiled. "I will."

"Thanks. I've got to go. Duty calls."

"Talk to you later, Cassie," I said.

"Later." The line went dead and I let go of the sigh that had been building in my chest.

"She hasn't heard from him, either?" Owen guessed.

I turned back to face the living room. Owen sat forward on the loveseat nestled by the fireplace, his elbows on his knees and his hands clenched together. I shook my head. "No."

Maximus stood suddenly, a growl rumbling from his throat. "I can't believe that feline bastard."

"We shouldn't jump to conclusions," I said. I'd defend my old friend until I knew for sure something was wrong. Though my talk with Cassandra had confirmed something was up with the panthers, it seemed like Jett was ignoring them as well. What did it all mean?

Where are you Jett?

Owen sat back on the leather sofa. "Let's calm down. We don't know what's going on with Jett. We're just riled up because of the waiting."

I groaned internally. The *waiting.* It was fucking agony. It had been hours since I messaged my friend on the NYC police force and still nothing. I knew we had to be patient, but it was getting harder and harder by the minute.

"I think we all know what's going on," Maximus rumbled.

My eyebrows furrowed. "What?"

"Jett is involved in this somehow. How else do you explain his sudden absence or string of suspicious behavior?"

"There could be a hundred things going on right now," I argued. If it weren't for Ariana, I might argue that Jett had a new woman in his life, and he was sneaking off to be with her. But though the panther alpha didn't want to admit it, I'd seen the look on his face when he first saw Ariana. He was as much hers as I was. He just hadn't accepted it yet.

"Clearly, something is up," Owen said. He stood, holding his hands out in a placating gesture. "But we don't want to accuse Jett of anything yet. Right, Maximus?" The bear alpha narrowed his eyes at the wolf.

I'd never seen someone more dominant than Maximus, but the second his shoulders slumped and he sat back down, I gazed at Owen in wonder. Did he realize what he'd just done?

"Let's all take a seat and stay calm. I'm sure we'll hear from your friend any minute, Cash." Owen sat back down, his foot bouncing anxiously despite the calm in his voice.

"You're right," I said. I slipped around the loveseat and joined Maximus on the long three-person sofa. "Any minute."

Owen smiled tightly and nodded. "Any minute."

12

ARIANA

You or them...

Jett's words echoed in my dreams along with a never-ending string of vampire attacks. I watched helplessly as every one of my mates was struck down, and I was all that remained. When the tears finally stopped and my inner beast burned for revenge, no matter how hard I tried, I couldn't call her. They were all gone. My beastie. My wolfie. They were stripped away from me, and I was left weak and alone. For all intents and purposes, I was human.

That's what Jett wanted me to do to the vampires, and after witnessing my mates sucked dry before my very eyes, I was tempted to let it happen. Let the vampires be wiped from this earth. If they killed my mates, I had nothing left to live for.

But before I could be released from my night-mares, there was one last thing my subconscious wanted me to see: the consequences of my actions. If I didn't listen to Jett, to Dr. Siegfred and the humans, not only would my mates be taken from me, but so would their clans. The bears would be wiped out. Owen's family. Maximus's pack, the wolves who welcomed me into their home, would be killed. The entire Dragon Council would burn, and the shifters of New York would be struck from history.

I squeezed my eyes shut and screamed, pouring the frustration I felt out of my lungs until my throat ached and I could no longer breathe. Only then did a light appear at the end of the tunnel, and my name was whispered on the breeze. Calling me... calling me...

Light burst before my eyes as I finally awoke from my nightmares. I was covered in sweat and panting like I'd just run a marathon. I pulled my legs up to my chest, taking deep breaths until the pounding in my chest slowed, and the bloody images in my mind faded.

I was exhausted. It felt like I'd been running all night. How was it possible that I was more tired now than before I'd fallen asleep? I sighed and closed my eyes.

"Ariana."

I jumped, my eyes wide as I scurried off the bed. Metal flooring burned my toes with cold, and I blinked in surprise at Dr. Siegfred standing next to my bed.

"Good morning," Muriel said, an amused smile on her face. "I didn't mean to startle you."

"Well, you did," I snapped, my throat aching. That colloidal silver was a real bitch.

"Apologies," Muriel said. "But I have a surprise for you."

I looked past the doctor to find a wheelchair sitting next to the open door. Two guards stood on either side of it, and I could see more through the door. "Where are we going?" I asked. This had *trap* written all over it.

"Like I said, I have a surprise." Muriel smiled and motioned for me to take a seat.

I looked between the doctor and the guards. Though I liked to think I made the choice to sit in the wheelchair and let them strap my ankles and wrists to it, there was no choosing. Either I did what they said, or I stayed in the small lab room and returned to my nightmares.

"Good girl," Muriel crooned. She took the wheelchair handles and turned me to the door, wheeling me out while the guards walked a few paces behind. "I want you to get a better idea of what we do here, and what we're working towards. I know you'll come around, even if it takes time. Maybe this will help push you in the right direction."

I rolled my eyes. I couldn't help it. They all wanted me to roll over and play dead. They wanted me to be their good little doggie, just like Dante had. My fingers tightened on the arms of the chair until they creaked.

I am no one's pet.

As long as I lived and breathed, I would fight for freedom. But for now, I'd play along. My mates would never give up. They were coming for me. I just had to survive until then.

Muriel stopped, and I heard a click as she locked the wheels of the chair. She walked around the chair until she stood in front of me. "I almost forgot." She produced a small spray bottle from the pocket of her smock. It was hardly the size of a tube of lipstick, but it held more power than my shifter body.

I recoiled at the sight and desperately called to my wolf. I heard the faintest of whimpers before one of the guards gripped my head and forced my mouth open. Muriel sprayed into my mouth once and then stepped back.

Pain lanced through me and poured down my throat like liquid fire. I groaned as it drained into my stomach, making me nauseous.

"Sorry, dear. Precautionary measure. You understand." Muriel unlocked the chair and continued wheeling me down the plain white hallway lined with guards at every other door. "We've been testing your blood," Muriel continued as if I wasn't in pure agony. "Very interesting results. We wanted to see what would happen to a vampire's blood if it came into contact with yours, and boy, was I surprised. When you take a look at your blood and a vampire's through a microscope, yours attacks the vampiric cells, consuming and replacing them with new, live cells. It's extraordinary."

My head spun as my body acclimated to the silver. Slowly, the world righted itself and the agony in my throat turned to a dull ache.

"Now, we weren't sure how your blood would react to shifter blood, seeing as your cells attack others," she went on.

I blocked out most of Muriel's ramblings until she mentioned experimenting with shifter blood. My body went cold as I thought of other shifters being kept here only to be injected with my blood. This was *sick*. And yet Dr. Siegfred spoke like it was the most exciting thing in the world.

"But when mingled with the blood of your friend, nothing happened." Her blue eyes blazed with excitement. "Literally nothing. I couldn't believe it."

Thank fucking hell.

"Blood of my friend?" I asked. My brain was still processing slowly through the fog that settled every time they hit me with silver.

"Your panther friend. Jett."

So Jett was allowing them to experiment on him now, too? I bristled. "And he *chose* that?" Despite the fact that Jett had put me here, part of me worried they had changed their minds about working with him and had thrown him into a cage somewhere.

He totally deserved it, but I wasn't so callous as to wish this on my worst enemy.

"Of course," Muriel said, like it was the most obvious thing in the world.

I sighed. *Of course.* Muriel continued her little speech as she wheeled me down a long corridor and turned into another. Suddenly, it occured to me that I was out of my room. I was one step closer to freedom.

My heart raced, and my fingers tightened on the arms of the chair. I tried to take a deep breath and relax through the endless monologue Muriel had prepared. I inspected the hallway as it brought back to mind the route we had taken. We had only turned twice, and I hadn't seen any exit signs or any windows. Did that mean we were underground? Or were they just keeping their super villain base windowless so I wouldn't try to jump out the first one I saw?

"We're here!" Muriel stopped beside a door identical to every other one in the long white corridor. She swiped her keycard over the panel next to the door, and it *whooshed* open. The doctor stepped through, pushing me in first while the guards crowded in after us.

The lights flickered on at our entrance to reveal another lab-like room. I blinked through the white spots dancing in front of my eyes until I could make out two different cells on the far side of the room. Both were like glass cubicles with another piece of glass between them. There was a commode in the corner of each, and a small cot on the other side.

"This is what I wanted to show you," Muriel said, her excitement increasing.

I shook my head. "I don't understand."

"I'll explain in just a moment, dear." Muriel locked the wheels on my chair, leaving me directly between both rooms so I could get a good look at their inhabitants.

I stared at the two people: both women, one human and one vampire. The vampire on the left looked ill, with graying skin and sunken eyes. She breathed heavily, something I was sure I'd never seen a vampire do before. Her brown curls fell lifelessly around her shoulders and in front of her face. She glared at Muriel, her red eyes filled with loathing.

I looked at the human, a young woman with pale orange hair, freckles, and vivid green eyes. She huddled on the corner on her cot, her thin arms wrapped around her legs. She didn't look sick like the vampire, but she was pale and trembled from head to toe.

"What's going on here?" I asked. The longer I looked at the two women, the more concerned I got. Cold dread pooled in the pit of my stomach until it formed a hard rock.

Muriel spun to face me, a controller of sorts in one hand and a clipboard folded under her arm. "Do you know Jade, Ariana? The human woman."

My eyebrows furrowed. Did I *know* her? I looked

back at the frail woman who had finally turned to us with wide, pleading eyes. "I don't think so."

"No matter," Muriel said. She stood beside me, a smile plastered on her face. "You *turned* this woman. Jade used to be a vampire."

I gasped involuntarily and swung my head around to face the woman. Her green eyes met mine, a thousand emotions rolling through her expression, the most vivid of them making me wince. *Hate.* This woman didn't even know me but she despised me. Had she really loved being a vampire that much?

"Do you know what happens to a cured vampire if they get bit again?" Muriel asked.

My blood ran cold. Both caged women tensed, fear written all over their faces.

"You wouldn't," I said. Finally, I understood. Doctor Siegfred had brought me here as a witness. She wanted me to watch her little science experiment, to see how my blood affected those who consumed it.

"It's all for science, Ariana," the doctor said. "It took us weeks to find one of the vampires who attacked you, and it was even harder to capture her. Now, we're ready to answer one of the questions that has been burning in the back of my mind."

I slowly peeled my gaze away from the cages to see the manic look in Muriel's eyes. She had no idea what would happen anymore than she did when she mingled my blood with Jett's. This could all go horribly wrong. I might not have read a lot, but I knew the story of Frankenstein. This was a dangerous game the doctor was playing.

"These are people," I growled. "You're hurting them."

Muriel scoffed. "They're safe as long as they're with us." She cut off my next argument with a flick of her hand. "There are three possibilities I believe have the most weight. One, the human who is bitten will be turned back into a vampire. Two, the vampire who bites the human will be turned human as well. And three, the vampire will die."

Before I could even process what she'd said, Muriel held up the controller in her hand and hit a button. A click echoed in the room, and the glass wall between cages receded into the back wall.

The vampire's eyes widened, and she flew to her feet. "Please don't do this. I don't want to hurt her."

I drew back in surprise. The vampire didn't want to hurt a human?

"Petra," Muriel scolded. "We've talked about this."

The vampire, Petra, pressed against the wall as far away from the cowering human as she could. Her breathing grew even more ragged as fangs poked her bottom lip. She groaned and closed her eyes, banging her head against the wall. "You're a fucking monster," she gritted out.

"Come on now," Muriel prodded. She seemed to be enjoying Petra's agony.

The vampire held her stomach and covered her

nose. I realized she was trying to block out Jade's scent.

"You must be thirsty, Petra," Muriel continued. "We haven't fed you in weeks. How can you resist your dinner?"

"Dinner?" Jade squeaked.

Petra glanced up. Her red eyes were hungry, and her skin was sallow. I'd never seen a vampires look so... ugly.

Muriel chuckled gleefully. "She's about to cave!"

I winced, fighting the urge to leap up and come to Jade's defense as Petra finally gave in. In a blur, she flew across the room and leapt on top of the human. The girl screamed as Petra sank her fangs into the side of Jade's neck. The vampire took a few pulls before leaping backward, slamming into the glass wall. She choked and spit, vomiting blood on the floor.

"She tastes like death," Petra hissed.

"Now, now, Petra," Muriel said. "You know that's not all you're meant to do. Turn her."

"What?" I snapped. My heart raced as I pulled at my restraints.

"*Turn her*," Muriel said again, more forcefully this time.

Petra looked from Muriel to the small girl groaning on her cot. "I can't," she said. "I promised I'd never turn anyone against their will."

"*Petra*," Muriel growled. "Turn her, and we'll give you real, uncured human blood. Don't, and we'll just get a more willing participant to replace you."

Petra blanched. I understood her pain and fear. If she refused, they might get someone violent who didn't care about humans to do the job, and her reluctance would be for nothing.

"Please let me go," Jade cried. Tears streamed down her cheeks, dripping from her chin. "*Please*. I won't tell anyone. I just want to go home."

Petra's lips parted soundlessly. I couldn't believe what I was seeing. This wasn't fair—not to anyone involved.

"Do it, Petra," Muriel snapped.

Petra grabbed hold of her hair, cradling her head in both hands. Muriel snapped her name once more before Petra flew across the room. She tore through her wrist with her teeth, sending blood spraying across the glass. Then she forced the wound to the human's mouth.

We all watched in silence as Jade struggled. A tear cut through the blood splatted on Petra's cheek, and she finally yanked away. Pressing her lips close to Jade's ear, she whispered an apology.

The human slumped against the wall, her eyes closed. This was what I was afraid of. What Muriel theories didn't account for—what if the vampire killed the human? Tears pricked the back of my eyes. How could they do this? How could they get away with this? The girl was *human* for fucks sake. Sure, she had been a vampire, but she was one of them now! Was this how humans treated their own kind?

Jade jerked on the cot. Petra took a step back, and I squeezed the arms of my chair.

Please be alive...

The whole cot shook as the human seized suddenly, shaking on the bed, foam dripping from her lips.

"She's dying," Petra cried, falling to her knees beside the cot.

"Help her," I snapped.

Muriel didn't even glance at either of us. Her eyes were glued to Jade as a *crack* echoed in the hollow space. I froze, my pulse thumping in my ears.

The human's once pale, freckled skin grew grey and hard. Strands of her orange hair began to fall from her scalp, slowly at first, and then in great clumps. Her hands gripped the metal edges of the cot, her fingers twisting and her nails blackening before turning into claws.

My mouth fell open as the once frail girl turned into a monster before my very eyes. It was like watching an old horror movie about Dracula, except Dracula was suddenly mixed with *The Thing*. The creature before me wasn't human, but it wasn't vampire, either. It was a hairless, gray thing with wide black eyes and elongated teeth too big for its mouth. Its body reshaped until its bones protruded, and it hunched over, vertebra jutting down its spine.

Petra was the first to move. She flew back into her own cell, a scream tearing from her throat. The monster turned its eyes on Petra, a thin white film like an extra eyelid blinking sideways over its lifeless gaze.

The monster reared back on its hind legs, which appeared almost broken and twisted backwards at the knee. It spreads its arms wide and screeched, baring several rows of teeth at us.

"Close the door!" Petra cried, cowering in the corner.

I looked between the vampire and the monster as it swivelled towards Petra, a growl rumbling from its throat. "Close it!" I screamed, yanking against my restraints.

Dr. Siegfred blinked as if out of a stupor and lifted the remote, hitting the same button she had before. The gate slowly appeared from the wall to close off the cells from one another.

The beast shrieked again, the sound grating against my ears and making me wince. It crouched, ready to spring, and then lunged into the glass wall. It growled and hissed and spit, raking its humongous claws across the glass as it tried to wedge its hands between the cells. But the door didn't stop, and the monster was forced to pull back.

My ragged breaths finally slowed as the safety wall clicked into place, blocking off Petra from the monster. Still, I continued to gape, unable to believe what had just happened.

Muriel turned from the cages, her eyes still bulging. "Well, I didn't expect that."

13

ARIANA

D r. Siegfred barely seemed to notice I was in the chair as she rushed it back to my room. I searched for exits all the way, finally seeing one down a long corridor that was more poorly lit than the rest of the lab.

"That was extraordinary," the doctor mused, but I couldn't tell if she was talking to me or the guards or herself. "I wonder if it does the same to all of them. I've never seen such a creature."

I tried to calm my hammering heart, shuddering at the memory of that beast throwing itself against the glass. Whatever it was, it sure as hell wasn't human, and it wasn't a vampire, either. I couldn't help but be even more relieved that my blood hadn't done anything to Jett's. Not that I'd expected it to. I'd fought lots of shifters, and I hadn't escaped without a scratch or two of my own. Plus, I was a shifter, so of course my blood wouldn't affect my own kind.

Muriel's trial to see if it would work on shifters concerned me more than the results. She'd promised me that first day that she only wanted to turn vampires human, but what if something could turn shifters human, too? What would happen when her organization decided another species was a threat? Were they really trying to eradicate all supernaturals—or at least hold the possibility in their power?

She deposited me in my room and promptly left, still marveling over the transformation we'd caused. I shivered at the thought, and then at the image of the grotesque monster that my blood had created. Even though the doctor had set it up and executed the plan, I couldn't deny that I'd played a part, however unwillingly. My blood was... Something worse than toxic. My blood had the power to do that to vampires, whether I wanted it to or not. It didn't just turn them human. It turned them monstrous.

Yes, the vampires who worked for Dante had been assholes, but then, I'd worked for Dante, too. No one under his employ had much choice in the matter. They'd taunted me cruelly, but was that worse than what I'd done? I'd killed for him—sometimes people of my own kind.

I began to pace the room, though I barely had the energy. Adrenaline alone fueled my agitation. Yes, vampires had attacked us several times. I'd killed them to protect myself and my mates. But I didn't hate all of them. After seeing Petra, it was obvious not all of them were evil. And after seeing the monster she'd created with my blood...

I felt sick at the knowledge of what ran through my veins.

The door popped open, and Jett strode in. My wolf awakened and whined pitifully, not understanding why our mate wasn't saving us from this hell.

Before I could stop them, words flooded from my mouth. "Jett," I said, my voice choked. "Do you know what the doctor is doing? She's crazy. You have to get me out of here."

Surprise flashed across his face. "What happened?"

"She turned a vampire into...into..." My breath hitched as the horror of the scene washed over me again, and my knees threatened to give way.

"Ariana," Jett said, using my name for once. He rushed forward, his warm hands closing around my upper arms. He held me at arm's length, and I found myself wanting to pull him closer, to curl into his strong arms. "What is it?" he asked. "Are you okay?"

For a long moment, we stood staring at each other. My heartbeat felt labored and funny, but my gaze stayed locked on Jett's warm, brown eyes. Suddenly, I wasn't sure it was just the silver making me weak.

Which was idiotic. This man was not my mate. He was the enemy.

"Of course I'm not okay," I said, pulling away. "I'm being poisoned, remember? And speaking of poison, my blood turns vampires into...monsters. Not just humans. I'm literally lethal."

Jett's lips pressed together. "I'm sure that's not true."

"Because you didn't see it," I said, sinking onto the edge of the bed. "You probably can, though. I bet the doctor is keeping her there to try some more of her sadistic experiments on her. She was human, Jett. And then she was..." I broke off with a shudder.

"It wasn't your doing," Jett said, taking a seat beside me and rubbing a hand gently over my back. "None of us can help what blood runs through our veins. You can't help that any more than you can help being a wolf, or I can help being a panther."

"You're right," I said, shrugging off his hand. "It's not my fault. It's yours."

I glared at Jett, and his concerned expression began to harden. My stupid shifter side felt a flare of disappointment, wanting nothing more than to connect with him again in whatever small way we had the moment before.

"I'll talk to the doc," Jett said, standing and moving away from the bed, his back to me. "She shouldn't have made you witness that. There's no need for it."

"No need for me to know what you're doing with my blood?"

"I didn't know it did that," Jett said. "I'm just trying to do what's right here, the same as you."

I snorted. "Holding me prisoner and dosing me with poison is what's right? Wow, Jett. Your moral compass never fails to astound me."

"Glad I can impress you so much," Jett said, pausing at the door and turning back to me. "And sometimes, Ariana, what's right for the greater good doesn't benefit one or two people along the way. Not everyone can win every time."

"I guess I'm the loser here," I said. "Thanks for the valuable lesson. I'll tell my wolf that next time she's crying because someone is shoving poison down our throat."

Jett's jaw tightened, and a pained expression crossed his face. "If you'd just cooperate..."

"I won't be complicit in what she's doing," I said. "Hell no. She's making something ten times worse than a vampire. Go see for yourself if you don't believe me."

"I might just do that," Jett said.

"Fine," I said. "Do it."

Shaking his head, he turned away and slipped out the door, disappearing into the corridor outside my room.

14

JETT

I stormed off down the hall feeling like the biggest jackass that ever lived. Yeah, Quicksilver was being a little childish, but I was no better. I'd fallen right into the trap of sinking to that level and arguing like a child. And worse, my fucking panther was going crazy with some instinctual bullshit about saving her.

No. We save the world first. Then the girl.

Even if I let her go, I knew Ariana wouldn't see anything noble in my saving her. And why would she? After what I'd done, after helping the humans bring her here, she had no reason to trust me or see anything good in me. And I had no reason to want her to.

I kept telling myself that as my phone buzzed in my pocket once again. I slipped it out and checked the screen. I had at least a dozen messages, most of them from Cash. Fuck. I saw a couple missed calls from him as well, but I didn't want to deal with them just yet. I had a message from Cassie that seemed a good alternative, so I held the phone to my ear as I headed for Dr. Siegfred's office.

"Seriously, Jett? You're going to disappear on me right now?" Cassie demanded in lieu of a greeting. "Clan business is going on without you. I hope you know that. Until you come back, I'm making all the decisions, and I'm not even sorry."

She paused to take a breath.

"Also, the otherpanther clans have been calling about our intention to join the American Panther Alliance. I was waiting for you to get back before I give them an answer, but since I don't know when that is, they'll probably just form without us."

"Fuck," I muttered.

"Or maybe I'll just decide for us," Cassie continued on the message. "That's my job as your Second, after all. Have fun in crazytown, or wherever you ran off to."

She hung up without a goodbye. I had arrived at the doctor's office, but paused to tap out a quick text before entering.

Tell them we're in. Can't leave just yet, but I'll be back soon. Thanks for taking care of things while I'm gone.

I sent the message, then made the mistake of tapping on Cash's message thread. There were at least a dozen messages. They wanted to know where I was and why I wasn't coming to help. They were on their way to find Ariana. They had traced the van.

Fuck. Of course they had. Some small part of me must have known they would, even wanted them to. Why else would I have given them the footage?

Still, I had thought the doctor would be able to replicate whatever it was in her Silver Shifter blood that made vampires human by now. I'd been counting on it. Now, all she had were a bunch of samples, not even enough to turn all the vampires in New York, let alone the world.

My frustration built until I wanted to slam my fist through the wall. Instead, I kicked open the doctor's door. She needed to remember that I was cooperating in all this, not that I was another one of her inmates. I could walk away at any time.

Except... She had Ariana. If I walked away, I couldn't take her with me. The humans had taken her. I'd just told them where to find her.

Muriel jumped and spun toward me, away from a film she was watching on her dual computer screens. In the video, I could see two beds set up, each with a woman sitting on it.

"Jett," Muriel said, jumping to her feet. "I'm so glad you're here. You won't believe what the shifter's blood did to that vampire-turned-human."

"Try me," I gritted out, crossing my arms and frowning down at her. She might be the one in charge here, but she was also just a human.

She didn't seem to remember that I could snap her in half like a twig if I wanted. That I was literally a predator in my other form, and she was prey. Her eyes gleamed with a manic excitement as she grabbed my arm and dragged me closer to her desk. "I can't stop watching it," she said. "It's the most incredible thing! It's something beyond what I'd even imagined. Not vampire or human, not shifter or witch, but an entirely new being. Her blood... It makes magic, Jett. She's— she's like a god! She's put a new species on this earth."

I didn't like the sound of this.

Behind her, on the screens, the vampire attacked the pathetic human on the other cot. I tore my gaze from it, disgusted.

"I brought her to your attention so we could turn vampires into humans," I said. "So they couldn't harm the shifter community or humanity. Not make some freaky aliens."

"But this is so much bigger than that," Dr. Siegfred cried, clasping her hands. "Don't you see, Jett? There are endless possibilities. We have no idea what her blood can do! Why, I haven't even injected it into an ordinary human yet."

The vampire on the screen returned to the bed, feeding the human her blood to turn her back into a vampire.

"And you're not going to," I said. "Her job is to cure vampirism, not to be your little lab rat for the rest of her life."

"Well, of course not," Muriel said. "But until we can isolate and identify the cure, she's going to have to keep making blood for us. You may have started this, but you can't stop it, Jett."

I couldn't answer. I was staring at the grotesque alien creature that had materialized in the glass cells on the computer screens.

I swallowed a wave of nausea, which hardened to an ember of rage in the pit of my stomach.

"You forced Ariana to witness this?" I demanded, turning away from the hideous scene. "You're one sick fuck, you know that, Doc?"

"She wasn't harmed," Dr. Siegfred said, scooting back from me as my hands balled into fists. "I know she's your friend. Or... Something."

I could feel my pulse throbbing in my temples as I took a step closer. My panther rose to the surface, pushing to be released on this helpless human, to make her pay for what she'd done to our mate. "How dare you bring that up?" I growled, my claws extending against my palms.

"I just—Look, she's fine," the doctor said, gesturing at the screens where she was wheeling Ariana from the room. "See?"

"She's not fine," I exploded, grabbing the doctor by the throat. I lifted her off the ground, my claws breaking the skin.

She shrieked, kicking her legs and clawing at my hand. I could feel my panther glowing from my eyes, and I knew that she realized at last how easy it would be for me to kill her. What she didn't know was how much control I had over myself. My panther was exactly as deadly as I let him be. If I wanted to show her a little of his presence, I might. But I hadn't lost control of him in almost fifteen years, not since my father died, and I wasn't about to start now.

I wanted to, though. Oh, yeah, I wanted to. I wanted to squash the doctor like the sick worm she was. But if I did that, maybe the humans would start looking for someone who could suppress shifting. I'd go mad with my panther trapped inside me forever. He was as much a part of me as my human side.

But I had opened a can of worms, and now there was no way to put them back. If changing the very nature of one being was an option, the only question was, which one would be next?

The thought doused my anger, and I dropped Muriel to her feet. She staggered backwards against her desk, her hand to her throat. I'd just barely drawn blood, but she stared with wide-eyed shock at her hand like I'd severed an artery. "You—you—" she sputtered.

"You have the rest of this day with Ariana," I said. "If you haven't figured it out by then, you're just going to have to find another solution. I'm taking her with me when I leave tomorrow."

"We only have a few samples we haven't used,"

Muriel managed, though she was quaking against her desk.

"Then take a few more," I said. "But don't even think about doing anything else to her. I'll be in the observation room watching you every second until then. If you lay a finger on her with the intent to harm... Well. You've only seen a glimpse of what I can do to you."

15

OWEN

"Owen, wake up," Cash growled inches from my face.

I blinked my eyes open. What the hell was going on? When had I fallen asleep? I slowly sat up, pushing away Cash's hands which had been shaking my shoulders. I sat forward and rubbed my forehead. I could feel a stress headache forming in my temples.

"What's going on?" I asked, my voice gravelly with sleep.

"They found out who owns the van. We have an address," Cash said. He darted

from the living room to grab his coat hooked on a coat rack next to the door.

"What?" My breath whooshed from my chest like someone had stomped on my lungs. My heart raced as

I imagined finding Ariana and holding her tight in my arms. Once we had her back I was never letting her go.

"Come on," Maximus barked. He bounced on the soles of his feet next to the door, his eyes wild with excitement.

I shot to my feet and grabbed my coat. Maximus had just wrenched the door open when a strange floral scent hit my nose, forcing me to backpedal.

Maximus froze, a snarl rumbling between his teeth. "Warlock."

I ground my teeth. This wasn't the time. Why did Dante have to choose *now* to make an appearance?

"Good afternoon, gentlemen," a chipper British voice cooed from outside.

I took a peek through the doorway to find Dante's minion standing a few feet away. He had a nasty smile curling his lips and deepening the wrinkles in his pale skin. His green eyes were so dark and his pupils so wide that his eyes were nearly as black as his suit.

"What do you want?" I snapped. I remembered this guy from the last time he threatened Ariana. He'd just shown up in wolf clan territory, getting right through their defenses to meet us at the main cabin. Only this time he was on bear territory. If he thought he'd get away with threatening my mate again, he had another thing coming.

The warlock—Nevil, I think frowned. "What a rude way to greet a guest."

"You're no guest of mine." I stepped forward,

towering over the small aging man with gray hair. "I think we made ourselves perfectly clear last time. Ariana belongs to no one but herself. You and your master aren't welcome here."

Nevil laughed. "You shifters need to learn some manners."

Maximus slammed his fist against the doorframe. If I wasn't in his way, I was sure he'd have landed his fist elsewhere—probably right against Nevil's snide mouth. "You chose a bad time to get in our way, warlock."

Nevil's laughter died. "It is you that has chosen a bad time to get in mine." His eyes narrowed at the wolf alpha. "It seems you've discovered the location of Mister Ryse's missing property. If you'll just hand over this information, I'll be on my way."

"You want us to tell you where to find Ari?" Cash asked.

"Like hell." Before I could stop him, Maximus was pushing passed me and lunging out the door.

Nevil's shape shimmered, and Maximus tumbled to the ground right through the warlock's form. He was only down a moment before his skin rippled and the scent of wolf filled the air.

"Maximus!" I warned.

It was too late. Human Maximus gave way to a large grey wolf with eyes like molten gold. His snarl ripped through the quiet yard, and then he lunged.

Nevil laughed as he teleported a few feet away. He

reappeared next to my truck parked in the circular driveway. "I planned on getting what I need peacefully, but if you insist on a fight, I'd be happy to oblige."

A tingle brushed my skin like it always did when a magic user was calling on their power. A growl of frustrated ripped from my throat as I dove out of the house and down the porch steps. Cash was quick on my heels, heat wafting off of him in waves.

"You're messing with the wrong alphas, warlock," Cash warned.

"Leave bear territory now, and you won't come to any harm," I offered. The warlock was only delaying us. Ariana was out there, and we needed to get to her.

The warlock shook his head. "It is *you* who should be afraid, shifter."

Flames blazed from the warlock's hand suddenly. They licked the air hungrily, growing until they stood two feet high. Orange light flickered in the warlock's crazed eyes. It was then I realized we weren't getting out of here without a fight.

If he wanted to face down three alpha shifters, let him. He'd be running with his tail between his legs in minutes.

Nevil took a step back and threw his fireball at Maximus. The wolf leapt out of the fireballs path, gaining ground on the warlock. Fire ate up the grass where he'd stood. I glanced at Cash to find him with a hand outstretched. He pulled the fire from the blackened grass and into his hand.

"You want to play with fire, warlock? Let's play." Cash threw the fireball right back at the warlock. Nevil's eyes widened as he blinked away. When he returned into sight, the fire he'd had in hand disappeared.

My heart raced as I realized what that meant. He might be able to teleport himself all around my territory, but he couldn't hold up another spell while he did it. If we wanted to win, we'd have to catch him right after he teleported.

"You can handle the fire, right, Cash?" I asked. My bear rumbled to life at my call, his massive form pushing at the boundaries of my mind. He was as ready as I was to take this bastard down once and for all.

"I got it," Cash yelled.

I smiled. Cash was a smart guy. He'd figure out what I had up my sleeve any second. "Watch our backs and catch him off guard." I didn't want to explain any further and risk ruining my plan. So instead, I let down the walls I used to keep my bear inside. My bear shot forward at my command, his fur enveloping my skin and claws pushing from my nail beds.

I let out a ferocious roar as I fell on four massive paws. I shook, letting my bear settle around me like a second set of skin.

Maximus and Nevil were locked in a constant battle of teleport and attack. Every time Maximus leapt forward to bite the bastard that dare threaten our mate, Nevil blinked out of existence and reappeared a few feet away, a laugh on his lips. But the second my bear's roar was unleashed, my clan would come running. Though it wasn't quite the same as the pack bond Maximus's wolves shared, I could feel their warmth and their anger as they finally sensed the danger in our midst.

Nevil teleported again, getting a little distance between him and the wolf alpha this time. I charged, my claws tearing up the lawn as I ran at him. The warlock blinked away once, then twice, as Maximus leapt for him. On the third time, he reappeared on the porch, and fire burned to life in his hands.

"I'm growing tired of this," Nevil said dryly.

"So are we," Cash snapped, launching a fireball of his own at the warlock.

Again, Nevil teleported away. Cash reigned his flames back in time to keep from ruining my house. I was grateful—my mother would never have let me live it down if we lost that house. It had been in the family for generations.

When the warlock came back this time, I was ready. I charged, a growl rising inside of me. I shot a look at Maximus as I went, and the wolf alpha braced his paws apart, ready to jump.

When Nevil disappeared this time, I skidded to a stop and threw myself around to face the opposite direction.

Maximus leapt at the same time I did. Just as Nevil

reappeared, the wolf alpha hit him hard, and they both tumbled to the ground. Maximus raked his claws down the warlock's chest, and I grabbed one of his legs in my sturdy jaw, biting down with as much force as I could muster.

A scream tore from the warlock's mouth, and then he blinked out of existence once again.

I waited, panting as I scanned the yard.

When the warlock didn't return after several moments, I slowly lowered my hackles and looked between the other two alphas.

"I think he's gone," Cash said. "That was a good plan."

I nodded awkwardly with my big head. It was always strange doing human things in animal form. I scanned the yard one last time before I sent out a quick message to my clan—or more like a feeling in our case. They were safe now, but they should remain on high alert just in case.

Maximus was the first to shift back, groaning as he stood. He returned to the porch and slipped on his jeans where they'd fallen. "Damn warlock," he muttered as he picked up the shredded remains on his black t-shirt.

I shifted back, my bear sliding off of my skin like water. I straightened and stretched my neck.

"What a coward," Cash huffed.

"Agreed," I said. "But he's gone now, and we've got to get going."

The other alphas froze. As their adrenaline faded, realization dawned on their faces. The warlock had just been a distraction. Now we had to find our mate.

"Let's go!" Cash called as he raced to his car parked at the end of the driveway.

Maximus was quick to follow.

I ran inside and snatched the first t-shirt and pair of jeans in my dresser, since mine had shredded when I shifted into a bear. I grabbed a t-shirt for Maximus before heading out the door to join the others. As I slid into the backseat, I tossed the second shirt to Maximus and began to dress.

"Let's find our mate," I said. My fingers curled around the backrests of either alpha as I leaned forward.

The engine roared to life, and Cash gripped the wheel so hard his knuckles turned white. He tore out of the driveway, sending gravel flying beneath his wheels. We hit the highway moments later, going far above the speed limit as Cash drove towards the city.

Soon, Ariana. We'll have you back soon.

16

ARIANA

A scream cut into my dream, yanking me from sleep. Despite the nightmares, I knew the scream hadn't come from me. The wailing rose and fell in an incessant drone.

I sat up, barely able to keep myself steady. Something inside me was straining to get out, like one of my beasts had awakened at the alarm. But when I reached for my wolf, she was as weak and injured as I was, and my dragon continued to sleep.

The previous day's events came back to me, and I immediately wondered if that inhuman beast Dr. Siegfred created had finally broken free. I slid my legs off the bed and took a few steps, my knees shaking with weakness and cold. I made it to the wall where the door always appeared, but there was no way out from this side. Shit. What if it had set the building on fire? I was trapped with only the hope that Muriel found me too valuable to lose.

And the hope that she hadn't been the first person the beast attacked when it broke out.

I pounded on the wall, though my cries were as pathetic as my wolf's whines by now.

To my surprise, the door slid back. I had been leaning my weight on it, and when it disappeared, I collided with a solid wall of muscle.

"Hey there, Quicksilver," Jett said, catching me in his thick arms.

"What's happening?" I asked, the shock of waking up to sirens and the fog of the drugs making my chest constrict with fear. My fingers closed around Jett's arms, clinging on. "Did that thing escape?"

"I don't know," Jett said, pulling me in and stroking my silver hair back. My wolf trembled with relief at this small comfort that had been withheld from her for so long. Our last mate had finally come to help.

"You have to get me out of here," I said. "It's our only chance, Jett. If you don't do it now, Dr. Siegfred will never let me go."

"I can't take you out just yet," Jett said. "But I will soon. I promise." His arms tightened around me.

"When?" I asked. "What if she turns against you, too?"

"She wouldn't dare," Jett said, his voice menacing.

"She would," I insisted with a shudder. "You didn't

see how crazy she got when she saw that human turn into... Whatever it was."

"I'm going to get you out real soon," Jett said. "For right now, I don't know what's out there, or why the alarms are going off. I'm just here to protect you in case anything goes wrong."

In case anything went wrong?

Anger rumbled up inside me, along with that uneasy feeling I'd had earlier, like something inside me wanted out. Was he fucking kidding me? Everything had already gone wrong. Nothing about this had been right from day one. And then I realized what I was doing, that I was clinging to Jett like he was my savior instead of my enemy.

Fuck that.

I was about to pull away when a realization dawned through my hazy, silver-soaked brain. Jett came and went as he pleased. He must have a keycard to give him access to my room. Which meant that maybe I could get out tonight after all.

Instead of drawing away and sniping at Jett, I turned my face up to his. "Promise you'll protect me?" I asked.

I could feel a slight vibration somewhere deep in his chest, like an honest-to-god purr. An instinctual response ran through me at the sound of my cat mate's pleasure.

"I'll protect you," Jett said, his voice low, smooth.

His fingertips trailed down the side of my face, his eyes intense on mine. I wanted to stay there in his arms, receiving this affection I had craved for so long. I didn't have to fake the pleasure his touch gave me. I closed my eyes and nestled against his palm, laying my cheek in his hand and turning my face up to his.

His breath caught, and after a second, his warm lips brushed mine. They were so soft that for a second I could only swoon against his hard body, every thought in my head vanishing like vapor. My mouth responded to his, reaching up, seeking the comfort and warmth and connection of a mate-bond. Heat wavered through my cold body, lodging between my thighs, and I moaned against Jett's mouth. His hand pressed against my lower back, securing my body against his, and his tongue slid between my lips.

The heat of his mouth startled me back to reality, and I realized I was standing in my room kissing the enemy while the building might be burning around us.

The anger that had stirred inside of me roared to life again, and I drew back slightly, breaking the kiss with a small gasp. Before Jett could speak, I gathered all the strength of that anger and drove my head up as hard as I could, slamming my forehead into his.

I was shocked at the force of the hit. I'd felt weak, like I might barely bump his head, but he flew back-ward, thudding to the floor flat on his back. My own head throbbed, but I rushed forward to crouch over Jett. I checked his pulse. Steady.

He was out cold, body slouched across the floor and head tilted to the side. My heart slammed in my chest, and my limbs trembled, some deep and primal energy running along my arms as if it were magma rising to the surface of my being. How the fuck had I summoned enough energy to knock out a huge man and throw him five feet backwards in the process?

I'd have to consider that later. Right now, I had other things to worry about. While the energy continued to rumble inside me, I might have a chance. I groped at Jett's pockets, finding his phone in one and his keys in the other. I yanked out the keys, but there was no keyhole in my door. Reaching under him, I slid my hand in his back pocket and pulled out his wallet. Flipping it open, I found a stroke of good luck for the first time since I had arrived in this place. The card was right in the front, as if he'd just used it—which he obviously had. I dropped the rest of the wallet and ran to the door. After searching for a minute, my heart was about to explode. There was no slot for the card!

Finally, I held it up, waving it slowly across the metal scanner next to the door. After a minute, a quiet beep sounded, and the door slid back into the wall.

"Thank hell," I muttered, stepping out into the hall.

The siren was even louder here, rising and falling with each wail. The bright, fluorescent lights that had lit the halls earlier had gone out, leaving blood-red emergency lights flashing in unison with the sirens. A chill ran up my arms as I looked up and down the dim, shadowy corridors. Taking a deep breath, I started in the direction we'd gone earlier, remembering the lone emergency exit I'd spotted on my way to the lab.

This place was a fucking maze.

Inching down the hall on my tip toes, I slowed to peer around the corner down the adjacent hall. Nothing. Not only was this place a goddamn labyrinth, but the guards were missing too. Normally, I'd find that comforting, but today, it scared the hell out of me.

A cold shudder ran down my spine and goosebumps pimpled my arms. I rubbed them for warmth, but the chill in my bones wouldn't go away. Something was wrong. The last time I traversed these halls they'd been lined with guards. Patrols had marched by and a man or woman clad in black stood at almost every doorway. But now? It was like a ghost town.

I sighed and inspected the hall one last time before I slipped past, heading back in the direction I *thought* was the lab where I'd witnessed the creation of a monster.

Though I hoped it was just a fire, or some kind of chemical hazard that started the alarm wailing overhead, I knew better. Coupled with the missing guards, I could only surmise that the monster had escaped and was wreaking havoc. What did they expect? It was a fucking *monster*. I'd never seen anything like it before, and I never wanted to again.

I continued down the hall until I reached another corridor. This time, I froze before I had the chance to take a peek. Copper assaulted my nostrils. It was a fresh and vibrant—definitely human.

I inhaled sharply and forced myself to look. Blood splattered the once white walls. Half a dozen bodies lie in varying positions on the laminate, their eyes unseeing and gashes torn through their clothes and flesh. Bile burned my suddenly dry throat, and I slowly took a step back.

There was no doubt in my mind that the creature had done this. The gashes were deep and ragged, like an animal had sliced through them. Blood oozed from the wounds and pooled on the floor. The wounds were fresh.

I stilled, my heart pounding erratically in my chest. If the wounds were fresh, than that monster couldn't be far. My gaze darted back the way I'd come, and then across the hall once more. Nothing moved.

I was safe for the moment at least. I took a deep

breath, trying to calm my racing heart. I had to remember where the exit was. That was my only chance. I closed my eyes for a minute and leaned against the wall. Pushing past the exhaustion, I tried to recall every step of my journey yesterday. The problem was, I had been too out of it to pay attention most of the way to the lab. So instead, I called to mind the trip back. I'd been shell shocked, but far more alert than I had on the trip there.

We'd continued down the main hall, but turned off several times. There was a left, and a right, and another left... I thought.

I groaned and opened my eyes. I just had to keep moving. I'd find it soon.

I faced the hallway with all the dead bodies and slowly made my way toward them. Blood overwhelmed my sense of smell and swirled inside my head. So much needless death, and all for a cure the vampires didn't want.

I held my breath and slowly stepped over the first body, and then the second. Before I reached the end of the hall, I realized there was no way to get around all the blood. I sighed. I'd have to walk through it.

Gritting my teeth, I stepped over the second to last body. Warm liquid squished between my toes and made me shiver.

I held my arms out at my sides, desperate to keep my balance. I took another step, and then another, trying to ignore the blood against my feet. When I finally stepped over the last body, only then did I look back.

Red footprints followed the path I'd taken to the end of the corridor, ending abruptly behind me.

As I glanced up from the dead bodies before me, I large shape caught my eye. I froze, and my blood ran cold. The monster stood at the end of the corridor, its lips pulled back to reveal row upon row of teeth. It opened its mouth wider, a long, hissing breath rising from its throat.

Shit.

My eyes widened, and my heartbeat sped as I stared down what was sure to spell my doom. There's no way I could fight that thing off. Not without my wolf or my dragon.

I desperately searched my mind for them. My wolf whined pitifully, and my dragon didn't even stir. I was alone without my beasties. And I was going to fucking die.

The monster raised its arms and let out an ear splitting shriek.

I slapped my hands over my ears, stars flying across my vision. My eardrums rang with the sound until I could feel it in my bones. Tears pricked the back of my eyes as pain split my skull, and then just as quick as it had begun, it stopped. I panted and opened my eyes—not having realized I'd closed them. The monster shot forward suddenly, almost blurring with its speed.

I yelped and backpedalled, slipping in blood and landing hard on my ass. "Shit!"

The creature flew over me. By some miracle I missed its lunge. I scrambled to my feet and did the only thing I could—I ran like hell.

My wet feet slapped the linoleum as I tore down the hallway back the way I'd come. I leapt over bodies and skidded into the left hand hall as another ear splitting screech echoed behind me.

Shit, shit, shit! I spun into the next hall and sprinted with every ounce of energy I had left. *Please, beasties, help!* I called to my wolf, and I called to my dragon, but neither could help me. My fists closed, nails digging into the palms of my hands.

I hadn't survived years upon years of captivity and torture only to be killed at the hands of some creature out of a horror movie. I wanted to fight. I wanted to kill it and rid the world of the monstrosity. But how could I when my beasties were silent and just plain human Ariana was all that remained?

A growl of frustration tore from my lips. Heat burned inside my chest, and an unfamiliar rumble echoed deep inside of me, one I'd been feeling for several days, urging me to fight though I had no strength. My steps faltered, and I slid into a wall. Pain shot through my shoulder, but I hardly felt it.

Something else had awakened in the depths of my mind, answering to my desperate call. Only, the rumble wasn't unfamiliar anymore, I recognized it just like I'd recognized my dragon the first time she'd shown up. Another beast had awoken to join the other two, and she was *pissed*.

The sound of claws scraping the floor brought me back to reality in time to roll away from the creature lunging at me.

I leapt back to my feet and opened my mind and body to my third beast. "Let's kill this bitch."

My human body was torn away, and in its place, a thick coat of fur extended over my skin. A cry flew from my lips as my bones and muscles shifted into something foreign. When the pain subsided, I was left staring down at the creature which had once been nearly twice my size.

I had huge brown paws tipped with razor sharp claws. I was a bear. A fucking bear! I couldn't believe it.

The monster screamed, and I looked up. A roar pushed from my throat, but the monster didn't falter. If anything, a challenge gleamed in its eyes.

Bring it on. If I died today, I was going down fighting.

The creature's back legs bunched, ready to lunge. Instinctually, I rose onto my hind legs, my arms outstretched. It leapt, sailing through the air, right into my chest.

Its strength pushed me back, but I rolled onto my side while binding it to my chest. I used my hind legs to claw at it while my teeth sank into its shoulder. It shrieked and struggled in my grip, twisting with surprising strength. This thing was stronger than a bear? What a load of horseshit.

I growled and held as tight as I could, but it snapped out an arm and sliced through my cheek. My grip loosened as pain cut through me. That's all the time it needed to wriggle from my grip and dig its teeth into my thick scruff.

Another slice of pain burned my neck, but it wasn't nearly as bad as the first. My fur was thick, and it'd take a lot for this thing to dig through it and find my throat.

I recoiled, yanking out of its grip and slammed my massive paw into the side of its head. The creature flew into the wall, its skull cracking against it. The wall caved in from the force, and plaster dusted the air.

I backed up, returning to all fours as the monster lurched out of the wall.

My chest rumbled with a threat. If it didn't back off, I was going to kill it. But the monster didn't hesitate. Any creature should have understood my warning, but not this one. It was as if Jade were compelled to keep attacking—or maybe it just didn't care.

It opened its mouth, and dark, almost black blood oozed from between its teeth, dripping down its chin and onto the floor. For some reason, I almost expected my blood to do something to it. Maybe change it back or kill it. But though it had a mouthful of my blood, it didn't appear any weaker.

I growled another threat. I knew my strength

wouldn't last much longer. Even if this new beastie had adrenaline working for it, I'd tire soon and transform back. Bear Ariana might be able to take this thing on, but human Ari would be dead in seconds.

"This way!" a distance voice shouted.

I froze at the same time as the monster. Footsteps thundered nearby. It seemed the guards had gotten together at last.

Something flashed in the monster's eyes. Hunger. It was going to kill them all if I didn't stop it. Though these people had caged me, abused me, and stolen my blood for their experiments, did they all deserve to die at the hands of this creature?

I shook my head. I was sure some of them had families, and I didn't want to take away the father or mother of a child, not like Dante had done to me.

I raced forward and slammed my shoulder into the monster's chest, throwing it off balance. While it teetered backward, I grabbed its arm in my teeth and threw it with all of my might into the wall.

The monster twisted mid-air, its clawed feet hitting the wall before it used its momentum to fly right back at me. It hit my neck with the force of a train, driving me straight through the wall into what appeared to be some kind of office.

It clawed at my stomach and bit at my neck. I struck with my hind legs until I threw it off. This time, I slammed my entire body weight against it, crushing it to the floor while I dug my teeth into its throat.

The taste of ash burst on my tongue, but I continued to press down until its flailing slowed, and then finally ceased.

I raised my large body from Jade's. It didn't move. With a heavy sigh, I backed up. My body was heavy, and I could already feel my bear slowly receding.

Not yet, I urged. Ignoring the pound of boots in the next hall, I turned and ran as fast as my bear could go. We took two turns before a sign caught my eye. *Exit*.

Relief coursed through me so intense I lost my grip on my bear, and she fled back into my mind. I collapsed onto my hands and knees, taking a few deep breaths before I climbed to my feet. I was almost there. Soon, I'd be free.

I forced myself forward one foot at a time until I could slam my hands against the door. I shoved it open. Cold night air pushed my silver hair over my shoulders. I breathed it in greedily as I let the door close behind me.

I froze as a familiar scent brushed my senses. Tears sprang to my eyes. There wasn't just one familiar scent, but three.

My mates had come for me.

CASH

I cradled a sleeping Ariana in my arms, holding her tight to my chest with everything I had. I lowered my nose to her hair, closing my eyes and inhaling her soft jasmine scent. My dragon nearly purred at the closeness of our mate. We'd nearly lost her.

The second my little Ari escaped the warehouse where she'd been kept, we'd all smelled her. We'd known she was near. I had run as fast as I could toward her. There was no creature on earth that could have stopped me from getting to my mate in that moment. As soon as I had seen her, relief had been plain on her face. She had collapsed in my arms, barely able to mutter out a few words before she fainted.

But those words had been enough. They echoed

again and again in my mind. I was sure they'd haunt me for the rest of my days.

Jett betrayed us.

There had been tears in her eyes, and they'd slipped down her delicate cheeks. I didn't say anything to Maximus and Owen until we'd returned to the car and were back on the road. They asked me over and over what she'd said. They wanted to hold her, too, but my dragon wouldn't let her go. *I* wouldn't let her go. Not yet.

Her soft breaths warmed my chest. I squeezed her tighter, but she didn't stir. Whatever they'd done to her in there, she was absolutely exhausted. I could smell the silver on her, and another substance—something foreign that made my dragon hiss and spit when he'd first smelled it. They had been drugging her for the entire time. It was the only thing that explained the fact Maximus couldn't reach her through the pack bond.

I sighed and brushed a stray hair from her face. Her plush lips were parted slightly, and her eyelashes fluttered like she was dreaming. Her skin was so soft and delicate. It was a wonder I didn't break her every time I touched her.

"Cash," Maximus growled.

I looked up, catching his eyes flashing molten gold in the rearview mirror. We were heading back to my penthouse. But after a quick discussion they had both agreed that the safest spot for Ariana was the closest one. She needed rest in a familiar environment. We'd decide what to do when Ari was feeling better.

Before then, I had to work up the courage to tell them. I had been wrong. It hurt to admit it, and not just because of my own pride. I had been a sort of mentor for Jett when we were younger. Though he'd cut me from his life, I had still believed in his goodness. Now, I felt wholly responsible. The others had believed Ari's distrust in him, but I hadn't. I had kept them from going after Jett, holding out when everyone told me he was involved. If I hadn't stood up for him, we could have gone after him sooner.

I sighed, closing my eyes and breathing in Ariana's scent until warmth spread through me. I forced myself to meet Maximus's gaze in the mirror. This was it.

"Jett betrayed us," I said at last. The words were like acid on my tongue. Even as I turned them over in my mouth, I wanted to spit them out and reject them. Jett would never betray us. Well, maybe us, but not *her*. Ariana was his mate, no matter how much he denied it.

"I fucking knew it" Maximus muttered. He twisted around in his seat, eyes narrowed as they met mine.

"Watch the road!" I snapped.

Maximus's eyes were still gold, but he slowly turned back around before we drifted into oncoming traffic.

"That's what she said?" Owen surmised. There was

no surprise on his face. I could see his mind working. He'd known all along. This had just confirmed it.

"Yeah," I said gruffly. I looked away from the bear alpha, and back down at my precious Ari. She was still sleeping soundly, despite our conversation going on around her.

"What does this mean?" Owen asked. "I had my suspicions, but I hoped they were wrong."

"You know that's what this means," Maximus growled. The steering wheel creaked under his iron grip. "This can't go unpunished."

Heat stirred inside me. I knew he was right. War against the panthers was the only answer. Their own alpha had betrayed the Silver Shifter. No one could get away with that—not even my young mentee.

"But, war?" Owen sighed and shook his head. "Is that really necessary? The Silver Shifter is meant to prevent wars."

Maximus slammed his fist on the dashboard. I stiffened, glaring at the side of his head from the back-seat. I knew he was angry—we all were—but he needed to contain himself. Especially in *my* car. "Of course she is, but we can't just let him walk away like nothing happened."

"What if Jett's people weren't involved?" Owen tried again. He was the most reasonable of us all, I realized.

Because no matter how crazy Maximus's words seemed, I was in complete agreement. Jett was no longer our ally, and he was certainly not my friend. A friend wouldn't steal away our mate in the dead of night. A friend wouldn't keep her from us for days and subject her to the Dragon God only knew what.

"He's right, Owen," I growled. My skin was hot and beading with sweat. Anger cut through me like a knife, stifling my airways until I could barely breathe. My dragon fought beneath my skin, ready to erupt and raze Jett's clan to the ground for hurting our mate.

I tried to take even breaths, to calm my beast from springing to life right in the back of my car. We had just left the city minutes ago and were certainly not far enough from traffic for me to turn into a dragon in the middle of the highway. I'd be outing us to the world, and what's worse, Ariana might get hurt in the process.

But I was just so angry. How could Jett do this? I'd called him my friend for decades, and he'd betrayed the four New York Clans for what? Money? Revenge? I had no idea what Jett was getting out of this. Guilt clawed through me. I should have known. I should have seen it sooner. My friendship with Jett had gotten in the way of my rational thinking. It blinded me to his treachery. Even now, all I wanted to do was make excuses for him. But I couldn't. Not anymore.

"Cash?"

I froze, then slowly looked down. Ariana's eyes were open slightly, hooded from sleep, but she was awake.

"Ari," I breathed out a sigh of relief and held her tight to my chest.

Her hands curled around my biceps, clinging to me as I clung to her. "You're hot."

I chuckled—I couldn't help it. "You're not too bad yourself."

"Cash," she chastised half-heartedly. "You're burning up."

The silence in the car was deafening. I was much older than anyone else in this vehicle. I shouldn't be losing my cool like this, but I couldn't help it—not after nearly losing Ariana.

I cleared my throat. "Sorry."

"You're not going to shift, are you?" Maximus asked, eyeing me in the rearview mirror. His eyes were no longer gold. Even he had gotten himself under control.

I avoided his gaze, instead holding Ariana's. Slowly, she reached up and cupped my cheek in her hand. A soft smile curled the edges of her lips. She was still half asleep as she leaned up and placed a soft, chaste kiss on my lips.

"I'm fine, Cash," she whispered. "Tell your dragon that. Tell him I'll be okay."

I nodded, enraptured by her silver gaze. I took a deep breath and closed my eyes, leaning my forehead against hers. *She's okay*, I told my dragon. *Our Ari is okay.*

I received a snort of dismissal before I felt the heat

recede from my skin. Whatever scales had formed disappeared, and by the time I opened my eyes, Ariana was asleep once more. I kissed her forehead softly and leaned back in my seat.

Our Ari was safe. At last. It was thinking about what happened next that worried me.

W hen we arrived at Cash's, he ordered Maximus to pull the SUV into the garage and close the doors before he allowed me out. I was a little surprised that Maximus didn't bristle at taking orders from the dragon alpha, but he did as Cash asked without comment. In fact, he'd barely said a word since we broke out of the lab.

Owen started to gather me in his arms, but Cash snatched me before he could. He slid from the car, scooping me up and searching my face with obvious concern. "Are you sure you're all right?"

"I'm fine," I assured him. "Just a little weak, but I can tell it's wearing off already."

I shuddered at the knowledge that if I was still in the lab, one of the nurses would be coming back to dose me again in an hour.

Not this time, I thought grimly. I was free, thanks to my mates and my bear.

My bear. Holy shit, I had a bear. That's what had been stirring inside my groggy mind, that primal fury wanting me to break free, to fight. I glanced at Owen, but before I could say a word to him, Cash had carried me to the elevator. Inside, he punched the button to close the doors, leaving Maximus and Owen to climb the stairs or wait.

"Someone's being a little possessive today," I said, smiling to let Cash know I didn't really mind. Not that much. In truth, I wanted to be around all my mates right now, but one of them was good if I couldn't have them all.

One of them who wasn't holding me hostage and forcefully subduing my wolf, anyway.

"When I was hurt, you took care of me," Cash said. "I'm returning the favor. The last thing you need is a bunch of over-eager alphas demanding your attention. And trust me, we would all be doing that."

"Instead, I get just one," I said, pinching his nose playfully.

"Nope," he said. "I'm going to insist that you to rest just like you did for me."

"That's no fun," I said with a pout.

"Now you know how it feels," Cash said with a chuckle as he carried me out of the elevator.

"I can walk," I pointed out, but I made no move to

separate myself from my mate. I wanted to be close to them as much as they wanted to be with me.

"You've been poisoned for a week straight," Cash said. "You need all your energy for healing."

"Surely you can put off tucking me into bed for a few minutes," I said, toying with the buttons on his shirt.

"I'll reserve an entire night for you," Cash said as he nudged open a bedroom door. "After you're healed. I wouldn't want you to feel like I'm taking advantage of you."

"You're not," I said, linking my arms around his neck and smiling up at him.

"You're right," Cash said, leaning down to lay me gently on the bed. "I'm definitely not."

He leaned down, brushing his soft lips across mine.

"I'm strong enough for more," I said, remembering how much Maximus had improved after our first mating. I wondered if it would work the same on me. If I took one of my mates to bed, would I awaken healed by morning?

"And you'll get it," Cash purred. "When you've had a night to recover. Believe me, I'm as anxious to be alone with you as you are. But we need you to heal and be at full strength, Ari. We don't know what tomorrow will bring."

I sighed. Sometimes being the Silver Shifter really fucking sucked. Unfortunately, I couldn't pick and choose when the responsibility would be mine. "You're right," I admitted.

"Of course I am," Cash said, nuzzling against my neck and inhaling my scent. I let my head fall back, sighing when his lips grazed my skin, sending a shiver through me. Cash's warm, bonfire smell surrounded me, and I sighed again, this time in contentment.

But too soon, he was pulling back and rising from the bed. He smiled down at me as he hooked his fingers into the waistband of my sweatpants. "What are you doing?" I asked, my breath coming quicker.

"I'm tucking you in," he said, slowly sliding my pants lower. I tried to swallow, barely able to contain the ache of hunger building inside me.

"That's all?" I asked.

"That's all," Cash said with a cocky grin. He tossed my pants into a hamper in the corner and reached for my shirt.

"You're evil," I said as he slid it off over my head.

"I know," he said, his gaze moving down my bare body in painfully slow strokes. When he'd reached my toes, he let his eyes travel back up my legs, lingering between my thighs until I had to press my knees together to stop the unbearable heat from making me explode.

"Be good," Cash said with a chuckle. He pulled the blankets up around me, leaned down to kiss my forehead, and snaked a hand under the blankets to slowly massage my nipple while his lips lingered on my skin.

"You'd better go," I said. "Unless you plan to stay."

"I'm going to fuck you so hard tomorrow," he whispered. With a grin, he straightened and said, "Goodnight, Ari." He strode to the door, then turned back with his hand hovering at the light switch. "Oh, and one more thing."

"What's that?" I asked when he didn't go on.

His green eyes sparkled as he smirked at me. "From now on, every time you tell me I only have one thing on my mind, I'm going to remind you of this moment when I was a true gentleman."

"Fine," I said, rolling my eyes. "But right now, I'm going to hate you for a few more minutes."

"Just as long as this one time lasts me the rest of our lives."

I couldn't help but smile as he switched off the light and pulled the door closed behind him. I sank down into the pillows, utterly exhausted despite my arousal. The fogginess in my brain had lifted, but my body felt like it had been run over by a bulldozer. Repeatedly.

My dragon was sleeping, my wolf was using all her energy to heal, and my bear was tired from the fight. My human body had spent a lot of time sleeping lately, but I was still drained from the ordeal. I closed my eyes and nestled into the soft bed, feeling my mates close by even though I could barely hear them as they talked in the sitting room. I let myself drift off into a comfortable sleep.

I JOLTED AWAKE. My heart was racing, and my limbs felt heavy despite the burst of adrenaline shooting through them. I blinked into the darkness, trying to calm my gasping breaths. My wolf whined piteously, dreading the moment she'd be poisoned again.

There's no one here. We're safe.

I lay back on the bed, kicking off the blankets. I was sweating from nervousness, from the nightmare I couldn't remember. I knew what it had been, though. It must be time for the nurse to come force silver down our throats, and my body had awakened in anticipation of the torture.

As I lay there trying not to panic, suddenly a warm rush of love flowed over me, as if we'd been dosed with the antidote to silver poisoning. My wolf instantly relaxed, lolling back and absorbing the wonderful sensation.

"Maximus," I whispered, closing my eyes and gripping the sheets.

A second later, the door opened and then quietly closed. "Ariana," Maximus said, lifting the sheet and sliding in next to me. He wore pajama pants and a T-shirt, but even through his clothes, his touch magic. Every part of me was instantly awake and wanting—no, *needing*—more of him. It was a craving I hadn't fully understood when Cash left me, but now that the drugs were wearing off further, I understood. I needed my mates. I needed them to heal. My wolf was frolicking up toward the surface, demanding time with Maximus's, but I held her in check.

"Cash is going to be mad that you're in here," I whispered, pressing my hammering heart to his.

"Do you think I give a single fuck about that?" Maximus asked, his voice a low, soothing rumble. "I heard your wolf crying. The only way to stop my wolf from answering that call is to kill me."

"Your dirty talk is so sexy," I whispered on a soft breath, wrapping my body so tightly around Maximus's that even he couldn't have pulled us apart. Not that he was trying. He rolled toward me, pressing his body against mine, burying his face in the hollow of my shoulder and inhaling deeply. A tingle of arousal flowed through me, blooming between my thighs like a flower.

"Your wolf has been weakened and injured," Maximus said. "Our bond will feed her and strengthen her."

"I feel so empty without their strength," I admitted, slowly grinding my hips against his. "Fill me up, Maximus. I want you inside me again. I need all of you this time."

"And you're going to get it," Maximus growled, guiding my hips as they moved. Wetness sprang to life between my thighs. He inhaled sharply when it soaked through the thin fabric of his pants to his cock, and the next second, I was under him.

"Max," I breathed. "Make love to me. No condom. Just us."

"Ariana…" he said, his eyes searching mine in the dark. "You're not ready for pups, are you?"

"It's safe now," I said. "It's not the right time. I won't get pregnant. I need to feel you, just you, inside me."

His cock throbbed against me, and I arched up, squeezing his hips with my knees. "I want that, too," he said, his voice hoarse with lust. "I want to feel you with my cock and fill you with my cum."

"Do it," I whispered, and the next moment, he'd lifted up and pushed his pants down. I slid my hands beneath his shirt, marveling at the ridges of muscle under his hot skin. He pressed the head of his cock to my slippery opening, a tremor of desire shivering through his body and into mine.

"Ariana," he whispered, his voice barely more than a sigh as he sank into me.

This was what I had been wanting, what I had been needing. Not to rest and be alone, but to be with my mates, to be close to them in a way I would never be with anyone else. As Maximus's strong arms caged me in, his body moving in rhythm with mine, I knew that this would recharge me in a way that nothing else could. My wolf was finally at ease, and my bear was growling for more. Even my dragon had begun to awaken from whatever toxin they'd been using to subdue her.

I was lost in the motion of Maximus's body atop

mine, his strong hips flexing as he thrust into me, the tight muscles in his shoulders as he held himself over me, the collision of his hot skin against mine. Only when I heard the door creak did I startle from the pleasure that had gripped me. My body tensed instinctually at the presence of another person, and Maximus sucked in a sharp breath as my walls clenched around him.

"Are you awake, Ana?" Owen's low voice rumbled as the door latched behind him.

Ana.

Owen had never used a nickname for me before, but I loved it instantly.

"Get the hell out," Maximus growled.

"Oh, shit," Owen said, backing a step toward the door.

"No," I said quickly. "Stay."

For a second, no one spoke. Even I couldn't believe I'd said that. But I knew as the words left my mouth that they were right. I needed my mates—all of them. The more, the better. I would heal so much faster with Owen here tending to my bear.

"What?" Maximus asked, looking down at me from where he was propped on his fists. His cock was thick and bare inside me, stretching me until I could hardly stand it. I wanted Owen just as much, though. After today, I knew that mating had unlocked my bear, and now it needed his.

"I need you, Maximus," I said, reaching up to caress his cheek. "But I need him, too."

"I can wait," Owen said, lingering at the door.

"No," I said. "Don't leave. I need you both inside me."

I could hear Maximus's swallow. "At the same time?"

"Yes," I said. "Are you okay with that?"

After a long moment, Maximus nodded. "Anything that's good for my mate makes me happy. If you care about them, then I care about them."

"And you?" I asked, reaching for Owen.

He approached the bed slowly, his hulking form a shadow in the darkness. His huge, strong hand engulfed mine and gave it a gentle squeeze. "I always want you, Ana. Every day, every way. Whenever and however you want me, I'm here."

I shivered at the sound of his new nickname for me, something that was just for us. "Let me taste you the way you tasted me," I said. I dropped his hand and trailed my fingers down the ridges of his abs.

"Are you sure about this?" he asked.

"I'm sure."

As Owen slid out of his clothes, Maximus leaned down to kiss me. "Let me turn you over," he whispered.

I knelt on the bed, leaning down to take Owen's thick cock in my hand. It was already starting to stiffen, and at my touch, it grew longer and harder until I couldn't close my hand around it. Maximus gripped my hips, positioning himself at my entrance. As I took Owen into my mouth, Maximus pushed into me from behind. I moaned at the amazing sensation of both men filling me to the brim at once. Owen's strong hands massaged my shoulders and stroked through my hair, and a groan of pleasure escaped him when I sank my mouth over his incredible length, taking him to the very back of my throat.

As I moved my mouth over Owen's cock, Maximus began to pump into me faster. I arched my back, spreading my knees, moaning at each delicious pinch of pain when he hit my depth. I bobbed up and down, marveling at the softness of Owen's skin against my tongue, at the roughness of Maximus's thrusts.

"I'm gonna come," Owen said suddenly, tightening his fist in my hair. Instead of pulling away, I mumbled a yes and sucked harder. Waves of pleasure rippled through me, and my own walls tightened around Maximus's shaft as hot, salty liquid filled my mouth. I gasped, an erotic charge shooting straight through me. An orgasm gripped my body, and Maximus groaned, slamming into me and holding me pinned against him as he flooded my core with his own release.

For a second, we remained as we were, locked together. When the last tremors had left my body, and I'd licked Owen clean, Maximus slowly drew out, and I rolled onto my side on the bed. Owen went to fetch a washcloth from the ensuite bathroom, and Maximus and I curled together on the bed. When Owen returned, he cleaned me up without a word, then slid onto the bed next to me. "You cool with me staying?" he asked.

"Of course," I said, pulling him closer. "If that's what you want?"

I wanted nothing more than to curl up between my two mates in complete bliss and fall asleep. I wasn't sure what they wanted, though. Inviting Owen to join us had been a spur of the moment decision, one I'd known in that moment was right, but I didn't know how much more he or Maximus was willing to give. After being alone, having no say in what happened to me, asking for both of their attention at once seemed way too demanding. What had been so natural the moment Owen entered the room, so natural that I'd had no doubt about it in the moment, was suddenly awkward in the aftermath.

"So, this is cozy," I muttered as I snuggled down between the two men.

"Ariana," Owen said with a deep, satisfied sigh. "You're incredible."

And just like that, I knew I wasn't alone in my contentment with the arrangement. I snuggled closer to his massive frame, feeling safe and protected with him and Maximus on either side of me.

"I think I can safely say the same for you," I said. "Both of you."

"I want to tell you something," Maximus said, his

voice serious. "Before you were taken, you said you loved me, and I didn't say it back. I don't want to go another night without telling you that I love you."

"Oh, Max," I said, my throat suddenly tight as I rested a hand against his cheek. His stubble was pleasantly rough against my soft palm, and I could barely contain my own emotion as I cradled his face in my hand. Of all my mates, he was the most reticent, and I'd never expected him to confess his feelings in front of another alpha. But he needed to tell me more than he needed to look strong right now. The fact that he could show his vulnerability in front of Owen made me love him even more. Maybe, just maybe, we really could be one big family. Somehow, this four-mate thing might work after all.

"I love you, too," I said, tears prickling my eyes. "But you didn't have to say it for me to know you love me. You've shown me in every single thing you've done since the moment we met."

I lifted my chin, and Maximus leaned in and pressed his warm lips to mine, tightening his hand around my waist.

"Except when he threw you in that cage," Owen said from my other side. I thought Maximus was going to jump over me and murder my other mate, but I pressed a hand against his chest.

"Except when you threw me in that cage," I said, smiling so he'd know I held no hard feelings about that. "I'll never let you live that one down."

"I guess you have to have something to hold over me," he grumbled, rolling onto his back.

"I'm kidding," I said, leaning in to kiss his bristly cheek. "I forgive you. If this is going to work, I'm not going to be keeping score or holding grudges against anyone."

"Just don't do it again," Owen said. "Or I might have to kill you."

"Ha," I snorted. "Don't count on it. If any one of you ever try to lock me up again, I'll be the one doing the killing."

20

JETT

I sat up and nearly doubled over from the pain battering my forehead. My hand flew to the goose-egg bump Quicksilver had left me as a parting gift.

"Damn it," I muttered, swiping my wallet from the floor beside me and checking to confirm my suspicion. I already knew she was gone. I would have felt her in the room with me. But I made sure the keycard was gone before pocketing my wallet, nonetheless.

I should have known she was tricking me. I was the last person on this earth Ariana would want to kiss. I had turned her over to these humans after all. And I couldn't expect the benefits that came with being her mate after I'd refused to accept that role. But damn, I'd wanted to kiss her. It was almost worth the concussion.

Fuck that. It had been more than worth it.

I turned to the door, only to realize I was locked in. The irony was not lost on me. I banged on the door, yelling until I heard footsteps in the hallway. The door slid open, and two guards blinked in at me. I pushed past them and ran down the hall. I didn't know how long I'd been out, but the sirens had stopped, and the hallway was in chaos. Bodies littered the floor, and plaster dust drifted down from holes in the wall and gritted under my shoes.

"What the hell happened here?" I demanded.

Dr. Siegfred scurried in my direction, her hair a tangled mess and her eyes wild. "She broke out," she said.

"I got that," I said, touching the lump on my forehead. "How? Where'd she go?"

"Some other shifters took her," Muriel said. "They must have heard about the blood, and maybe they were afraid it would work on them, too."

"Shit," I swore under my breath. I knew exactly which shifters had come for Ariana, and they couldn't care less about the lab. They'd come for their Silver Shifter.

"When she came running out..." Muriel began, then shook her head. "You didn't tell me she was a bear! We only had her wolf and dragon subdued."

"A bear?" I said. "Huh. I didn't know she was that, too. That means she's most likely a panther, too..." My panther purred in agreement, showing me how appealing he found that idea.

"What? Why?" Muriel asked, looking confused.

"No reason," I said with a shrug. "She seems to be any kind of shifter she wants."

Any kind of shifter that's her mate.

Maybe that was how it worked. Maybe she couldn't be a panther until I'd claimed her as my mate. Not that it mattered right now. Ariana was with the rest of the alphas, which meant she would have told them everything by now. Fuck. My clan was about to have war declared on it...by every other New York clan at once.

One of the guards shifted and cleared his throat. "Would you like us to keep looking, Ma'am, or stay near you?"

"Continue the search," Muriel said before turning back to me. "Another small problem, I'm afraid."

I crossed my arms, squeezing my fists to hold in my frustration. "A small one? Because if it's not of major importance, I've got some things to do back at my clan headquarters."

"Well, see, that altered vampire woman, she was in a glass observation cell."

"And?"

"And it was shattered during your friend's escape."

"So, now we've got a vampire-curing shifter in danger from the vamps, who won't want to leave her alive. At least here, she was protected. We're never going to get another chance with her." My panther let me know his displeasure with that theory by mewling like a kitten.

"We have plenty of extra samples of her blood," Muriel said. "We should be fine."

"I don't care about her fucking blood," I said, my claws extending from my fingertips. "I care that they're going to find her and kill her."

"Oh," Muriel said. "Well, of course. There's that, too."

"She's got three super pissed off, super powerful mates, and they're going to be after both of us," I said. I didn't mention that they'd be especially angry at me.

"We'll be safe here," Muriel said, but she glanced around as if regretting she'd sent her guards away.

"And we've got this weird-ass Nosferatu vampire-hybrid creature running around New York," I finished. "We have no idea what that thing wants, or what it's capable of, or even what it is. I think it's safe to say your little scheme to protect humans has not been a success. Now, if you'll excuse me, I have a clan to protect right now. If you need me, you know where I'm at."

I gave her a mock salute and hurried down the hall. Ariana had left my phone, so I flicked it on as I stepped over collapsed sections of wall and made my way out of the building. The lights in the parking lot illuminated my car. Well, at least they hadn't been so hell-bent on revenge that they'd slashed my tires.

Still, I approached with caution, scenting the air to make sure no one was hiding under it or ready to ambush me from behind the building. When I didn't find anything suspicious, I climbed in the car and clutched the steering wheel. After a second, I leaned forward and thudded my skull against the wheel. What had I done? I'd only wanted to get rid of the threat to our clan, but I'd managed to make enemies of every single pack in New York—including my own.

Instead of uniting the clans and working with the Silver Shifter, I'd had her kidnapped and experimented on. The experiment had failed spectacularly, and I'd probably fucked us all in the process. My clan was not going to be safe from vampires. Not only were the vampires still here, but I didn't have the support of the three other New York Clans to help me fight them the next time they attacked.

The gravity of the situation sank into me, weighing me down until I could hardly lift my hand to put the keys in the ignition. But I couldn't run from this. I was the clan's alpha, and it was time to go home and face my mistakes. The consequences could be dire. I might have to send some of the families away so the other clans wouldn't annihilate our population. The other alphas would fight my pack if it stayed in New York, but they wouldn't hunt them down to kill them if they left. Except me. They'd probably hunt me down.

And with good reason, I thought as I eased my car along the streets of New York. I wasn't going to run. New York was my home. I'd been born here, and I'd die here. Instead of going into hiding, I would die fighting, like my father had. But first, I had to get the other panthers out of here. This wasn't their fight or their mistake. If the other clans attacked, there would be casualties— probably a lot. Together, the three other clans could wipe us out. It wasn't fair to ask the panthers to fight the other clans, to risk their lives, for a mistake that their alpha alone had made. Sure, some of them would do it. Most of them would if I asked. That's what clans did.

What alphas did was protect their clans. I'd failed with the vampire extermination idea, but I wouldn't fail this time.

When I arrived back at my apartment, I wasn't even a little surprised to see the light on. I opened the door and stepped inside, my hands already raised in surrender. To my relief, it wasn't Cash here to rip my throat out, although that was almost as bad as what I found. Cassandra was sitting in my recliner, tapping her artificial nails on the table as she stared straight at me.

"Before you say anything, I need your help," I said.

That melted the grimace from her face. "What?" she asked, sitting up straight. "This must be serious. What happened? Everything okay?"

"No," I said, sinking onto the edge of the couch. And then I told her. I told her everything, from the moment I met Ariana and my panther started insisting she was my mate, to the moment I'd tipped off the humans to her location, to the moment she'd smacked me in the head and knocked me unconscious. When I finished, I raised my eyes from my linked hands.

"I thought I could get rid of them once and for all," I said. "For all the shifters in New York, but especially for Dad."

Cassie sat silent for a long moment. At last, she sat back in the chair, shaking her head. "Man, you are so dumb."

"I know," I said. "But I think it would be best if you took the rest of the clan and left for now."

"We aren't leaving you in New York by yourself, Jett," she said. "No matter how many dumb decisions you make, you're our alpha."

"Except you shouldn't have to stick by me when I make decisions like that," I said. "It wasn't in the clan's best interest."

She squinted sideways at me. "Yeah, but in your own dumb way, you thought it was. It's not like you deliberately set out to hurt the clan."

"Yeah, but I did hurt them."

"Yeah," she said slowly. "You made a mistake. Everyone does that, Jett. Even alphas."

"You wouldn't have made this mistake," I said, my shoulders slumping in defeat. "Or the one that lost the last alpha."

Cassie stared at me, her eyes narrowing. "I wouldn't have made this mistake, that's true," she said. "But negotiating with the vampires for a hostage?

Yeah, Jett, I would have made the same decision you did."

My eyes snapped up to meet hers. "You would?"

"Of course," she said. "That was a no-win situation. From the moment Dad got captured, we'd already lost. If we'd gotten him back, and fought on the vampires' side, we would have lost a lot more than just Dad. You made the decision an alpha should make. You put the clan above your own personal needs—even your family."

"I can't believe you're not scrambling to take alphahood from me," I muttered. "I'm practically begging you to take over the clan and move them out of New York."

"And I'm saying no," she said. "You're being a good alpha, and I'm being a good Second. My job is to talk you out of your asinine ideas. If you'd let me do that before, we wouldn't be in this situation."

"You're right," I gritted out. "So, now I'm asking you for advice, as my Second."

"You don't need my advice," she said. "You know what to do. We need all four clans to fight the vampires. You're the alpha. Make it happen."

"There's no way they're going to talk to me now," I said. "Even if I apologize, they won't listen."

"Well, you have an instrument that's supposed to bring the four clans together," Cassie said. "So, I suggest you start there. Not to mention she's your mate. Not that I care about that, because I don't. If you don't want to take a mate, it's none of my business. But she is the Silver Shifter, so you'd better get ready to pucker up those lips because you're going to have to suck up like you've never sucked before."

"Ariana's not going to want me as her mate anymore," I pointed out. "Not after what I did. She'll never trust me."

Cassie rolled her eyes. "We both know it doesn't work like that. If she's your mate, neither of your cats are going to stop until you share the mate bond. Mark my words, Jett. Let your panthers lead the way, and it'll happen."

21

ARIANA

The next morning, I lay on the bed between Maximus and Owen, my head cradled on Owen's arm. I didn't think I could get any happier. My wolf and my bear were snoozing in bliss inside me, and my human was just as content lying between these two amazing men. The sheet lay over our three bodies, and it was all I could do not to lift it and peek underneath again. I couldn't believe this was real, that I could feel this good again after what had happened to me over the past week.

When he saw me stirring, Owen nuzzled into my neck, his beard tickling my skin. Maximus lay facing me, his fingers tracing slow circles around my belly button, sending shivers of ticklishness through my satisfied body. To my relief, I felt so much stronger than I had the night before. Like always, my beasts had known what I needed before my human brain had realized it.

"How long have you been awake?" I asked, looking from one of them to the other.

"We didn't want to wake you," Owen said.

"Or leave you," Maximus said. "You needed your rest."

"So, are you okay with this now?" I asked at last. "You're not upset about sharing me with Owen?"

Maximus's serious eyes searched mine. "I know I don't always do the right thing, or show it the right way, but I always want what's best for you, Ariana. I want you to be safe and happy above all else."

"You're still unhappy about the four mates thing?"

"No," he said. "When you were gone, I saw how much you meant to the others. As much as you mean to me. I know I'm not the smooth-talker, but that doesn't mean I don't care about you."

My heart filled with love, and I lifted my hand and laid it gently against his cheek. "I know that, Max. I've never doubted it."

"Good," he said, leaning in to press his lips to mine.

"Me, too," Owen said. "I love you, Ariana. You're my mate, and I'd do anything for you. I love seeing you happy, no matter who you're with. I especially love that I'm one of the men who can make you feel good."

"Yes, you did," I said, snuggling against his massive, naked body. Maximus scooted in, sandwiching me between himself and Owen. Just when I thought we might be ready to start all over, a tap sounded on the door.

Before we could answer, Cash's grinning face poked in. "Ari, I was just going to—"

His voice cut off mid-thought when he caught sight of the three of us lounging on the bed.

"Oh," he said, his smile faltering, replaced by a look of surprise that was nothing short of comical. "If I'd known you were up for this..."

"I didn't know I was, either," I said. "Until it happened."

"Come in," Maximus said. "You don't have to stay out there. We all want to be near our mate right now."

"Really?" Cash asked, his face lighting up.

I shot Maximus a smile that was full of all the gratitude and happiness I felt at seeing him coming around and understanding that all my mates needed me as much as he did. I snuggled closer into his arms, relishing the strength of his body against mine under the sheet.

"There's room right here," Owen said, scooting away from me just enough to make a space for one more person. "Don't worry. I won't bite...this time."

Cash looked a bit startled when Owen shot him a wink, and I couldn't help but laugh. After a second, Cash bounded over and crawled into the spot beside me, though he remained on top of the sheet. When Owen snuggled in behind him, I realized that my animals were wrong—it turned out, I could be even happier than I'd been a minute ago.

"So, I had this theory," Cash said, not seeming to mind how close Owen was staying. "Maybe you have to claim a mate before you can shift into their form."

"Yeah, but I tried to shift into a bear before," I said.

"Huh," he said, frowning a bit as he stared at the ceiling. "That's true."

"But I do have another theory," I admitted. "It seems like... I first shifted into a dragon after we had sex. I couldn't shift into a bear then because I hadn't with Owen. But now..."

"That's not surprising," Maximus said, propping his head on his hand and looking down at me. "Wolves' true mate bond is not final until the pair have mated. This makes sense. When you've truly claimed a mate and formed a mate bond, you gain their ability to shift."

"And whatever other abilities they possess," Cash said. "Strength for the bear. The mental link and communication you share with Maximus. And dragon fire—I bet you can throw it with your hands in human form, like I can. I'll teach you how."

"The only question is," Owen mused. "Which gift is your Silver Shifter gift? The ability to shift into any of your mates' forms, or the ability to turn vampires human?"

After a minute of musing, none of us could answer that question.

"I don't suppose you'll be shifting into a panther anytime soon," Maximus growled. "Not after what Jett did. It's too bad you won't get the power of invisibility, though. That would be useful when the vampires attack next time."

"Of course not," I said. "I can't take a mate who betrayed me like that." The animal part of me protested at the sound of my denial. She didn't care what Jett had done. To her, he was our mate as much as the others.

"No one expects you to," Owen said, a frown darkening his brow.

My beasties growled for her last mate again, but I told them to kindly shut up while I addressed the mates who had actually cared about me and protected me all this time. "What are we going to do?" I asked. "He's one of the four New York alphas, but obviously he's not on our side."

"We can't let him get away with what he did," Maximus growled, his arm tightening protectively around my waist.

"Agreed," Cash said, his mouth set in a grim line.

"Really?" I asked, pulling back to look at him. "I mean, he's your friend..."

"He *was* my friend," Cash corrected. "He's made it clear that friendship no longer exists. He let us all know what side he's on. Every shifter knows that you never mess with another man's mate."

"Even if that mate is yours, too," Owen murmured.

"You're all in favor of punishing Jett?" I asked, looking from one to the next.

"Aren't you?" Cash asked.

"I don't know," I admitted. "What are you going to do?"

"We have to declare war on his clan," Maximus said. "He left us no choice."

"He did almost the exact thing the vamps did to his father," Cash said. "When they killed his father, we joined forces with his clan and fought the vampires. Now he's kidnapped you. He knew what the consequences would be."

"Isn't his clan the smallest of the shifter clans in New York?" I asked.

"Yes," Owen rumbled. "It wouldn't be difficult to drive them out altogether."

I lay there thinking for a minute. At last, I shook my head. "No. I don't want to do that."

"Ariana," Maximus said. "What are you proposing?"

"My job is to unite the clans," I said. "Not to run one of them out. I know we can't trust Jett, but we can't take it out on his clan. We can't punish them for being panthers just because their leader is a dick. That's just as unfair as punishing all vampires for being vampires."

"Okay, no war," Owen said. "What's the plan, then?"

I realized then that he cared what I had to say—

they all did. They were waiting for my input. They would respect what I wanted, would value my decision above all else. If I wanted war, they'd declare it. If I didn't, they wouldn't. As satisfying as it would have been to make Jett pay for what he'd done, I knew that revenge was not the answer. I was going to have to be the bigger person and forgive Jett.

I wasn't ready to do that just yet, but I didn't want his panthers to be harmed, either.

"I want to make amends," I said. "But don't worry, I'm not stupid. I'm never trusting that feline bastard again."

22

ARIANA

Finally, we're heading home. I blinked in surprise as the thought flickered through my head. I wasn't sure when wolf territory started feeling like home, but after all I'd been through in the last week, I wanted nothing more than to be home with the wolves. Something about the pack lent me a sense of peace. As soon as we crossed onto pack lands, I could feel it—the excitement of our return thrumming through the bond.

The pack was happy to have us back, which surprised me a little. The last time I'd been in close contact with Shira and the others, they'd hated me. They were pissed that Maximus wasn't my only mate. I understood that. Maximus was their alpha and seeing him—feeling him—unhappy was hard.

But the feeling of contentment that drenched my mind the moment we returned told another story.

Maximus was okay with our situation, and I was welcome here. I was part of the pack.

I stared out the window until we pulled up in front of the main cabin. Wolves poured out of the front door before Maximus had even turned off the car. Shira was first to my door, wrenching it open so hard the joints squealed.

"Ariana!" Shira cried. "You're okay!"

The wolves' second-in-command took my arm and helped me out of the car before enveloping me in her arms. I blinked stupidly, totally shocked. Out of everyone, Shira was the last person I thought would greet me so warmly. She'd been angry when I saw her last.

"I'm sorry," she whispered, her breath hot against my ear. "I'm so sorry. I'm glad you're okay."

Shira pulled back, holding me at arms length. Her lips twisted in a small, careful smile, and her eyes shone with guilt. Did she think this was somehow her fault? I understood why she'd shunned me. It had hurt, but I'd understood it.

"Thank you." I smiled tentatively, not sure how to precede. This was unfamiliar territory for me.

Shira nodded and stepped aside, allowing Owen to take my arm and guide me into the cabin. Pups scurried around my feet the second we stepped inside, and I would have tripped if it wasn't for Owen's quick reflexes.

"Welcome back!" said a woman from the pack. A

few others approached us with welcoming smiles before allowing us into the living room to sit down.

Even after a day of rest, I was still tired. The silver and whatever they were giving me to hold back beastie were almost out of my system, but not entirely. Maximus said the silver should be gone by tomorrow, and Cash was sure I'd be able to go dragon-mode when I needed to. Looked like I wasn't getting any fireball throwing lessons for another day.

It felt good to have my beasties back, and I was proud to have a third joining my little tribe. My mind felt full, though my heart was still missing a piece. Jett hadn't just betrayed me, he'd betrayed the New York Clans. I didn't want anyone to suffer, and that's exactly what would happen if I let my mates have their way. They wanted blood. Retribution. I might be pissed as hell had Jett, but I didn't want him or anyone else to suffer. He was still my mate, and these were still my people. I was glad they'd sided with me in the end. The panthers wouldn't suffer, but something would have to be done about Jett eventually.

"How about we have a barbecue tomorrow, and let Ariana get some rest today?" Maximus suggested, his voice booming over the ruckus the pack was causing.

There were a few disappointed groans, especially from the whining pups, but after a few minutes of corralling, the wolves had left the building. I was left with my three mates in relative peace.

I sighed and leaned my head against Owen's shoulder. We'd sat down on the three-person sofa, and Cash immediately took the place beside me. I reached through the bond to see how Maximus was feeling. There was a twinge of annoyance, and a sliver of jealousy, but nothing more. He'd finally come around to this. Maybe that's why the pack was so happy to see me. Did they sense that we'd finally put jealousies to rest?

"It's good to be home," I said. "I missed this."

"We missed you," Cash rumbled, a heated look in his eyes.

I turned my gaze on him, my beasties stirring to wakefulness. They understood the look in Cash's eyes just as well as I did. A smirk curved my lips, and I reached for my dragon mate. From the look in his eyes, he hadn't forgotten his promise for today.

Cash took my hand, and I pulled him forward until our lips met.

His skin was hot beneath my fingertips, and his scent enveloped me. Suddenly I was surrounded by the smell of bonfires and cinnamon, and I kissed him greedily. Owen's grip on my shoulder tightened, and he drew me against his hard chest, his hands sliding down to my hips.

Heat began to build in my core until a screech broke the stillness of night.

We all froze, our ragged breathing the only sound.

"What the hell was that?" Cash asked as he leaned back.

I stared into his green eyes, his confusion reflecting my own. Panic shot through the pack bond like a splash of ice.

"Something's coming," Maximus warned. He raced for the door at the same time I leapt out of Owen's lap.

I followed on my mates' heels into the front yard. Trees were silhouetted against a brilliant moon hovering in the starry night sky. The forest looked utterly still until a car came flying from between the trees.

"Scatter!" Owen shouted.

I dove to the side, the sedan just barely missing me. It slammed into the grass beyond the front porch, metal grinding and glass shattering upon impact.

I sidestepped the wreckage and peered into the trees. Where the hell had that just come from? One of the other lodges on the mountain? I hoped no one was hurt. Through the bond, I couldn't feel anyone injured —just panicked—but still, we had to protect the pack from any danger.

"What's going on?" Cash snapped.

"Who's on my land?" Maximus shouted into the trees.

Another screech filled the night, somehow sorrowful and enraged at the same time. My skin crawled, and a shiver descended my spine.

"I smell a vampire." Owen cursed under his breath and took a half-step in front of me.

Right now, I wasn't sure how well I'd do in a fight with only my bear at full strength, so I didn't protest.

"Fuck," Cash growled. "What should we do?"

"I won't leave my pack," Maximus said firmly.

"Of course we won't," I said. "I only smell one vampire."

Owen nodded. "Just one."

"Then I say, bring it on." I smiled until another screech sounded closer again.

Through the trees, a female figure appeared, tall and slender with wild blonde curls and stunning blue eyes ringed in red. Fury twisted what I thought might be a beautiful face, turning it into something ugly.

Owen sucked in a breath. "The Lamia Queen. Helena."

Cash's mouth dropped open. "Seriously?"

I had no idea what the fuck was going on, or who this queen was.

"You!" the queen screamed.

I barely blinked before the woman appeared before me. She grabbed my throat and slammed me up against the side of the cabin, stunning me senseless.

"You did this to her," Helena screeched. Tears leaked from her bloodshot eyes, creating tracks down her flushed skin. "You took my love from me!"

What the hell was she talking about?

"Let her go," Cash demanded. I could feel his heat

even from a few feet away. He was moments from transforming and burning this vampire to a crisp.

"Your blood is toxic," Helena raged at me, ignoring Cash entirely. "I should have had you killed long before now. It was silly to think you weren't much of a threat, and now she's gone. Your blood turned her into a monster!"

My eyes widened and my heart stopped. Jade. The human at the lab. The monster Petra was forced to create. That was Helena's mate?

I am so fucked.

"I'll kill you for this!" Helena's grip tightened painfully.

A wicked growl sounded nearby, followed by the tearing of clothes and flesh. By the time I looked over Helena's shoulder, Maximus was in wolf form. He lunged at the Lamia Queen's back, but Helena simply raised a hand, her fingers splayed.

Magic burned through the air, and Maximus froze mid-leap, his jaws wide open. I looked between my mate and Helena, my blood running cold.

"You won't live to see the dawn, wolf." Helena flicked her wrist, and Maximus flew backward. She yanked me back from the wall, and suddenly I was flying through the air.

I felt weightless for a good long moment, my body travelling high in the air from the force of Helena's throw. I searched my mind for my dragon, but she groaned in reply, still trapped inside of me by whatever drugs had poisoned her. I tried to spin my body as much as I could, but by the time I saw the ground, it was coming up at me fast.

This was going to fucking hurt.

To be continued...

∼

Follow Ari and her mates in the next installment, coming June 2019.

∼

Can't wait for book 4?
Read on for a short excerpt of Alexa's Chasing Her Cats (a dark RH) and Katherine's Demon's Game Novella (a paranormal RH).

A NOTE FROM THE AUTHORS

Whether you enjoyed *Silver Shifter: Her Bear* or not, please consider leaving a review on Amazon, and/or Goodreads! Every review helps get the book in the hands of new readers, and is extremely helpful!

Thank you so much for reading, and we hope to see you again in the next book!

Chasing Her Cats
A Dark Reverse Harem PNR

Alexa B. James

PREVIEW

CHAPTER ONE

Itzel
Princess, Ocelot Nation

From my position behind the dense shrubbery, I eased my head up just enough to take stock of the enemy. Ducking down quickly, I flattened my back against the prickly bushes and waited, blood thudding in my ears, the darkness ominously quiet around me. When no shots came, my eyes swept back and forth along the line of crouched warriors. "Ready?" I whispered, slotting the ammunition into my blowgun.

My team followed suit. When all guns were loaded, I waved my arm to signal them to move out, and they scrambled from seated positions to crouched and ready for action.

"Charge!" I screamed, leaping to my feet and

clearing the shrubs in a single bound. Battle cries rose up around us as my team barreled onto the field, and the enemy scrambled to avoid being shot. I blew the dart from my gun, swerved to miss an opponent, and kept running. I had to find another hiding spot to reload, or I'd be vulnerable to attack.

"Itzel, you devil," Tadeu cried, leaping after me. His fingers snagged at the ends of my black hair, but I wrenched free, ignoring the sting in my scalp. I leapt over another hedge only to hear footsteps heavy in pursuit.

Shit! I kept running, swerving down a narrow, shadowy lane. It lay abandoned to the night, like everywhere else in the kingdom. No one else dared break the king's weeknight curfew. Only the faint glow of paint on the toes of my shoes provided illumination. I darted through the streets where I'd played as a child, my footsteps echoing behind me as I ran. Pausing at the end of an alley, I flattened my back against the wall, my heart pounding with exertion.

I slid my feet from my shoes, meaning to pick them up and sneak on silently. But a pursuer's footfalls alerted me he was near, so I abandoned my shoes and darted out into the empty street. I streaked across, digging into my pocket for the keys I'd nicked from my father's chambers before heading out that afternoon. I doubted he'd missed them—or me—that day.

Keeping my blowgun in one hand, I shoved the circular key into the indentation on the arena's door.

The door gave way with a groan, and I flinched at the sound. Without checking for a pursuer, I slipped into the inky blackness within. Feeling my way with my bare feet, I sidestepped along the wall until I found the tunnel that led onto the arena floor. I heard the door scrape behind me, followed by loud whispers.

Shit. There were several of them.

I darted forward, praying a janitor hadn't left a bucket or other random item in the tunnel. Hard-packed dirt greeted my feet as I reached the main floor, and a grin spread across my face. The quiet patter of my footsteps on the ground echoed off the high ceilings, but I couldn't afford to stop now. I ran at breakneck speed across the floor, counting on the echo to throw them off.

I ran smack into a pile of hay. Bundles topples in front of me, and I went sprawling on top of them, rolling to the floor on the other side.

Heart slamming, I scrambled around into a defensive position. Lying in wait, I raised my blowgun to my mouth and inserted a paint-dart. I was ready.

A footstep sounded somewhere in the arena, the soft padding almost inaudible. I tensed, straining my eyes against the darkness, my ears against the silence ringing inside them. Not another sound.

Where were they?

Suddenly, the rustle of hay sounded just behind me. Before I could twist around, strong hands grabbed my shoulders, forcing me to the floor. I struggled, fighting to stay silent as he pressed my face into the straw.

"Gotcha," a rough voice murmured in my ear.

"Tadeu," I growled, bucking under him. "Took you long enough."

He crushed his body onto mine, pinning me with his weight. "Itzi," he purred. "Game's up, Princess."

"I thought you'd never catch me."

"But I did," he said, his calloused fingers sliding under the edge of my shirt, skimming along the band of my shorts. "Are you my prize?"

"You wish," I said, my breath quickening as his hand slid under me, pressing against the front of my shorts. I could feel his hard length pressing against my ass as I struggled.

"Why not?" he asked. "How long are you going to make me wait?"

"We're in an arena with at least one other player," I said. "Not now."

"I'm starting to think you share your father's opinion of me," he growled, his fingers biting into my mound.

"I don't," I shot back. I squirmed against his fingers, but they only worked my shorts further into me. "How could you think that?"

"Maybe a stable hand isn't worthy of Her Grace's cherry," he said, slipping a skillful finger under my shorts, tapping my clit through the layer of silk beneath.

"Of course you are," I said. "And don't call me that."

"Why not? You are a princess, aren't you?"

I snorted. "Try telling my father that."

"I don't have to," he said. "He reminded me just the other day."

"What?" I asked, finally twisting my body free and rolling over to face him.

"He's noticed that we still spend time together," Tadeu said bitterly. "He told me we should have outgrown these games, and I shouldn't indulge you." He slithered onto me, pressing a thigh between mine. "And that if I had too much time on my hands, he'd send me elsewhere, where someone could keep me better occupied."

"No," I said, gripping the corded muscles of his arms. Tadeu was my childhood best friend, my first kiss, my first and only love. As soon as my sister took the throne, I was going to convince her to let us marry. Father had laughed at me when I'd asked, but I'd been only a child then. I hadn't dared ask once I'd been of marriageable age. Father would never allow such a disparate match, even for a human daughter like me. My sister, however, could be persuaded.

Tadeu slipped his fingers under the edge of my shorts again, this time beneath my damp panties. "What's it going to be, Itzi? Are you going to give it up at last, or am I going to have to dream of your tight pussy while I fuck a stable maid against the barn wall again tonight?"

"Poor tragic Tadeu," I said. "At least you get fulfillment every night."

"I can fill you full every night," he said, sliding his finger into me.

I gasped and arched up, stifling a cry when I saw a paint splatter glowing like stars on another player. I bit down on my lip, holding in a moan of pleasure as Tadeu's finger pumped into my wetness faster and faster. I squeezed my knees together, increasing the pressure on my clit. He pulsed his finger inside me, and a tiny whimper escaped my throat. Seconds later, a paint dart burst on my chest.

With a cry, I released Tadeu's hand. He chuckled and drew away, flicking on a flashlight. His accomplice, Josue, stood grinning a few paces back.

"You cheater," I cried, punching Tadeu furiously in one solid pectoral. "You just got me going so I wouldn't run while your partner snuck up on me."

"I could have just held you down and called for him, but this was more fun." He popped his finger in his mouth and sucked greedily. "Tastes like cherries."

"Stop calling it that, or I'll give you a taste of my fist."

Josue was laughing his ass off. "Rejected again," he hooted.

Tadeu stood and offered me a hand, which I

slapped away. "Have fun with your stable maid tonight. Too bad you can't get anyone better."

"Says the woman who begged me to fuck her the day I first kissed her."

"You're a horrible, vulgar man."

"The best kind to fuck."

Continue reading today!

http://amazon.com/dp/B07MQYX4VP

Demon's Game

A Paranormal Reverse Harem Novella

Katherine Bogle

PREVIEW

(Series Coming Soon)

CHAPTER ONE

*I*f this guy touches me one more time, I'm going to fucking lose it.

My fingers tapped impatiently against the sleek wooden surface of the bar as I stared down the lecherous fool sitting across from me. He wasn't the first to hit on me tonight—not by a long shot. Working at a bar in downtown New York City wasn't an easy gig, but it was helping me pay my way through school.

Now if only this guy would order his drink and get out of my space, I could go back to stressing about my final project.

"*Clarrera,*" the drunkard slurred. He hadn't been able to say my name right for three drinks now, and if he didn't get his hand off my wrist, he was going to wind up losing his front teeth. Then he'd *really* have trouble pronouncing my name.

"It's Clara," I said, forcing a pleasant 'I-want-to-keep-my-job' smile. "What can I get for you, sir?"

For the third time in as many minutes, I tried to pull my hand back. And again, his sweaty fingers tightened on my wrist. I winced. His grip was starting to hurt. I was definitely going to have bruises in the morning.

The drunkard leaned in close, pulling me as close as I could get while still having my feet on the ground. His hot, whiskey-heavy breath bathed my cheeks, and turned my stomach. *No, no, no! This was way too close. Way too fucking close!*

"What's a pretty girl like you doing behind the bar?" the man asked. He stared pointedly at my cleavage, which due to the awkward position he'd forced me into, strained against my black work-shirt. "You should have a sugar daddy taking care of you." He chuckled and grinned so wide he flashed yellow teeth. "Why don't you let daddy take care of you?"

I shivered. "Sir, I have a job to do. If you'd release me, I can get you another whiskey."

He frowned; probably irritated that I was ignoring everything he said. "*Clarrera*, come here—"

"Clara!"

My heart skipped and my tensed body finally relaxed a fraction. I'd never been so happy to hear Eli's singsong voice in my life. My favorite co-worker appeared at the door to the back, a brilliant smile on her gorgeous, tan face. Eli beamed at the drunkard pulling me halfway across the bar. His eyes went wide, and his mouth dropped open. Eli had that affect on men.

While he remained in a stupor, I took my chance to extract myself from his hold. Once I was free, I backed up until my ass hit the display against the wall, sending rows of wine glasses rattling.

"Oh, you're with a customer!" Eli gasped with fake surprise. Her cherry lips popped into a small 'o'. "So sorry, sir! I'll let you finish with Clara-dear." Again, she flashed a smile that could light up the whole room.

The drunkard still hadn't recovered, though his eyes were definitely roaming down Eli's curving body. Even in a polo, slacks and a matching black apron, Eli could still stop traffic. Maybe it had something to do with her flaming red hair.

A sliver of jealousy twisted in my gut. I could only dream of having curves like Eli. My slight figure, straight black hair and grey eyes were boring in comparison to the fiery vixen.

"It's no problem," the drunkard finally managed.

I took a deep breath to gather myself before pouring the man a whiskey. As soon as my obligation was fulfilled, I excused myself.

Eli raised an eyebrow at my approach, and I quickly pulled her toward the back door. We'd worked together long enough for Eli to know when I needed a minute.

"You good?" Eli whispered. She took my hand and

squeezed firmly. Though she had an innocent, flirtatious vibe only moments ago, the rage in her blue eyes spoke danger. If that man had hurt me, Eli was about to go all 'hell hath no fury' on his ass.

I forced a smile and nodded. "Yeah, I'm fine. Thank you."

Eli let go of my hand. "Anytime. You know I've got your back."

"I know."

Eli glanced over my shoulder as she pushed open the swinging door to the back room with her ass. "Enrique, can you handle the bar for a few?" she called inside.

An answering grunt confirmed our fellow bartender would cover for us.

Eli flashed a cheeky smile as she grabbed my wrist and pulled me into the break room. The smell of pizza sauce and burnt dough filled my nostrils. Enrique must have blown up another pizza pocket in the microwave.

I bit my tongue on a groan. Guess who was going to have to clean that up? Definitely not Enrique.

Once we were inside the break room, Eli threw herself down on the worn brown sofa, laying her arms over the top of the cushions. "What's up, girl? I haven't seen you in a few days."

I sat down on the armchair closest to the door and ran a hand through my long black hair, tucking it behind my ear. "I've been busy with school. My final project is due next week."

Eli rolled her eyes. "It's always work with you. Do you ever take a break?"

My lips pressed into a firm line. We'd had this conversation many times before. "I'll take a break once I'm done the semester. I have to be on my A-game, or I'll fail this project and have to retake the entire year."

Eli leaned her head back against the couch and groaned. "Clara, you know I love you, but you have to learn to chill out. Being high strung is only going to raise your blood pressure."

I bit my lip. "Like I said, once the semester is over—"

"Are you off tomorrow?" Eli sat forward, leaning her elbows on her knees.

I blinked in surprise at the sudden change in topic. "Yes..." I replied slowly. I didn't like where this was going.

"Great!" Eli bounced off the couch and grabbed her gold clutch from her locker. When she sat back down, she held out three black envelopes with golden script on the front. "You're going to take these off my hands then."

I looked between Eli's face and the cards. Eli pushed them forward, waving them around until I plucked them from her hands. "What are they?"

"Three invitations to an *ultra exclusive* party outside the city." Eli grinned wickedly and wiggled her eyebrows meaningfully. "I work tomorrow, so I can't make it. I want you to have them. *Use them.* Invite two of your girlfriends along and make a night of it." She leaned back against the couch and crossed one leg over the other, looking far too pleased with herself.

"Eli, you know I can't. I have to work on my project." I turned over the invitations in hand. I knew Eli meant well. She always did. But Eli was a free spirit. She didn't understand commitments or work ethic. I sighed and set the invitations in my lap. I pulled one of the cards from its envelope. The invitation was beautiful, the same matte black as the outside with a crisp golden border. I scanned the invite for the location, but I didn't recognize the address.

"*Clary,*" Eli said, using her nickname for me to try and sway me. "Please? I don't want these to go to waste. You'll have all day to work on your project, and then you can take a town car to the party. It's already paid for."

I chewed on my lip. "I don't know. I really wanted to hunker down tomorrow."

I'd been working on my final project for weeks—or at least I'd been trying to. I still haven't come up with a final design for the pretend start up company I'm supposed to be creating a media packet for. If I didn't finish the logo design soon, I wouldn't have time to complete the rest of the material required.

"It's *one night.*" Eli raised her eyebrows as she leaned forward and took my hands. "You'll be back to work by Saturday morning. You'll have *loads* of time to finish before your shift on Saturday night."

I narrowed my eyes at her. Though Eli had asked if I worked tomorrow night, she'd already known—especially if she knew I worked Saturday. Still, it did sound like fun. The invitation said to *dress to impress*. There was an open bar and free food. What more could I ask for?

"Fine," I said.

Eli's eyes went wide. "You'll go?"

"I will. But you have to promise me you'll lay off after this. No bugging me to *chill out* until after finals." I glared at the petite woman.

Eli held up her hands in a defensive gesture. "Of course! No more nagging, I swear!" She motioned a cross over her heart, and grinned from ear to ear. "I'm so excited for you!"

"Yeah, yeah." I rolled my eyes. She just thought I was going to get laid. That was another one of her issues when it came to my social life. If I wasn't getting any, then I wasn't really living—at least according to Eli.

"Call your friends! I'll head back out there." She hooked a thumb at the door and stood, adjusting her shirt and slacks.

"Thanks, Eli," I said, driving as much sarcasm into those two words as I could.

Eli snickered all the way back into the bar. Only when the swinging door outside closed did I relax.

My co-worker was right about one thing. I could use a break. I couldn't even remember the last time I'd done something besides work, or go to school... and work some more. Damn, was my life really that dull?

Continue reading Demon's Game in the Of Lore and Legends Anthology!

https://www.amazon.com/dp/B07NVJJTXG/

ABOUT KATHERINE BOGLE

Katherine Bogle is the bestselling author of the steam-punk phenomenon, QUEEN OF THIEVES, as well as the international bestselling DOMINION RISING series.

She first found success with her debut novel, Haven, which came second in the World's Best Story contest 2015. Since then, she has gone on to release 11 books with one core theme: kick-butt heroines. Though her series may span genres—from fantasy, to steampunk to science fiction—she will always write about strong women overcoming the odds.

Join her newsletter for info on upcoming releases, free stuff and more:
https://www.subscribepage.com/p200e3

Follow Katherine for all the latest updates:
katherinebogle.com
AuthorKatherineBogle@outlook.com

ABOUT ALEXA B. JAMES

Alexa B. James is the adult romance shared pen name for 2 USA Today Bestselling YA authors.

The Alexas love coffee and romance novels of every variety (why choose?). Their plans for world domination include writing more books that make your pulse pound and your heart sing.

Join their newsletter for info on upcoming releases, free stuff and more:
http://eepurl.com/dvkHYv

11531775R00136